Blood Bound

Book Two of the Blood Match Series

Melinda Call

Blood Bound, Book Two of the Blood Match Series

First edition

ISBN: 979-8-9883767-5-0

Cover art by Megan at CryoMerch

Editing by Brandi at My Notes in the Margins

Acknowledgements

This book is dedicated to my wonderful husband, Russ. His encouragement of my writing career has made this book possible. Thanks to this patient man, so many plot and character issues have been resolved during hot tub brainstorming sessions. His love and support have kept me going when imposter syndrome sets in while still reminding me it's okay to take a break sometimes. Thank you for being my rock and biggest fan.

My editor, Brandi from My Notes in the Margins, provided thoughtful notes to help polish this novel. Thank you for correcting a major old wives' tale that would have made more than a few readers pull their hair out. I'm glad she wasn't scared away by the darker content and continues to help make these books shine.

My amazing daughter, Megan, contributed not only the cover art but content suggestions. She may never see Rowan as I do but she loves him just the same. Her love of this world keeps me motivated to continue to create more stories. More of her work can be found at CryoMerch.com.

Chapter One

Things are rarely as they seem. I once believed immortality would calm the maelstrom of fury that plagued me when I was simply a vampire. Not that I was ever simple; a sixth-generation vampire is nothing to sniff at. Life had always come easy for me: my career as a defense attorney, financial security, and anything else I've ever desired. With one glaring exception.

"And to that end, the firm has decided a leave of absence would be best, Mr. River."

Hearing my name yanked me out of my own musings. "Excuse me. Did you say leave of absence?"

My boss placed the papers he had been shuffling into a neat pile and looked me straight in the eye. "An *extended* leave of absence."

Slowly, I pulled my arms back from where they had been resting on the table, sat up straight, and placed my hands in my lap. My knuckles cracked as my hands closed into fists. Red momentary flooded my vision as I imagined closing my fingers around that idiot's throat.

"May I ask why?" My tone and volume were not to my liking so I cleared my throat and started again. "I've only just returned."

"Victor, in the month since your return, you've had one client leave in tears, a couple filed a restraining order against you, and yesterday I received a call from Judge Henry regarding an incident with his bailiff." He unnecessarily smoothed his silk tie as if contemplating his next words. "If it were anyone else, I would not be suggesting a leave of absence, I would be firing them. You have two choices. Take the proffered leave or clear out your office."

He stood and I knew the matter was closed. My eyes roamed the conference room searching for support but no one would meet my gaze. The only person that would have backed me up was lying cold in a cemetery across the valley, by my own hand, but that was ancient history.

In the year and a half since my rebirth, more and more decisions had been forced upon me. I was now one of the most powerful beings on this planet but was being treated like a bratty twelve-year-old girl. When had I become such a pushover? This was going to stop and stop now.

My boss lingered as if he wished to say more in private. Fishing my phone out of my jacket, I pinged my secretary stating we needed to address my calendar as soon as I finished this meeting. I rose as the last person left the room and quietly closed the door.

"Victor," my boss's tone indicated sympathy, but he reeked of fear. "We don't want to lose you but we feel you need more time to deal with your… accident. Perhaps a change of scenery?"

He rested his hand on my suit jacket sleeve but when I looked down at it, he pulled away as if burned. While few knew the details of my transformation, anyone who had an ounce of awareness could sense the air of a predator.

Ironically, I was looking at one of the most vicious attorneys in LA. Many would consider him the predator but, in his case, his actions were limited to words and judge rulings. I was something far more sinister and he knew it.

My eyes bore into his while keeping a cool detached expression then I slowly smiled. "I believe you're right. Maybe I did jump back into the game too soon. Actually, I've been thinking about visiting family up north."

A flicker of surprise flashed across his face before he too smiled. "I'm glad you're taking this so well. Contact me after the holidays and we can discuss your future here at the firm."

There was a significant chance that if he had attempted to shake my hand, I would have torn his arm off and beat him with it. Instead, I nodded an agreement and left the room. My petite secretary jumped up and followed me into my office as I walked past. While she looked about nineteen, she understood the consequences of me having to ask twice. I settled behind my desk and logged onto my computer.

"Deborah, work with Mr. Dennis's secretary to have all my current cases reassigned," I began without taking my eyes off the screen.

The leather chair squeaked as she shifted nervously. With a sigh, I turned to look at her. How she could even sit in that tight skirt was beyond me.

"Mr. River, your cases have already been reassigned," Deborah nervously admitted.

Once again, I was being forced toward an action. I smiled genuinely at her and she visibly relaxed. Deborah had been one of my better secretaries. Here was a woman who knew her place, always looked impeccable, and never questioned me unnecessarily. In a perfect world, she would have made a very nice mistress, if not a little too breakable for my liking.

"I'm taking a leave of absence for my health and would like you to arrange my travel. I'll be visiting my baby sister in Montana through the holidays. I'd like to leave no later than Tuesday but need a couple days to make arrangements for my house and the like."

"Of course, and your return date would be?" Deborah asked.

I turned to face her fully and folded my hands on my desk. "Let's just leave it open ended for the time being."

A flicker of disappointment crossed her pretty face. She subconsciously tucked a wayward strawberry blond curl behind her ear. She'd changed her hair recently and was still getting used to the new length. While nervous habits like this normally drove me nuts, today it was strangely endearing.

"Deborah, words cannot convey how much I appreciate all your hard work. I'll do everything I can to make sure the firm keeps you on during my leave. They would be fools to lose someone of your caliber." I added the tiniest drop of persuasion into my words.

Her green eyes widened and a flush crossed her creamy cheeks. "It has been a pleasure to work with you too."

A laugh escaped before I could stop it. "I believe you are the first person to say that and while I don't believe you, I'll accept the compliment. To show my appreciation, I'd like to invite you to dinner at my house Sunday night. Modesty aside, I'm almost a better chef than lawyer."

Again, she tucked the wayward curl. "Dinner isn't necessary, Mr. River."

"Victor, and I insist. For the time being, I'm no longer your boss so we can dismiss the formalities."

This time there was no blush and she leaned forward. "Then dinner it is. I'll bring wine. Red or white?"

"Red, of course."

Chapter Two

The line for some new dance club stretched around the block as I waited for the stoplight to change. Scantily clad and overly made-up bimbos giggled while wannabe players polluted the air with cheap cologne. My Z3 whipped around the corner and I left those imbeciles behind without a second thought.

I guided the black sports car into the underground parking garage about half a block past the club. The alarm chirp echoed as I headed toward the private elevator. As a newly converted immortal, I had to check in regularly and approve travel with my clan. Laws and protocols had to be followed or chaos would rule. That didn't make it feel any less like checking in with a parole officer twice a month. The more I thought about this forced leave of absence, the more I warmed to the idea. At least in Montana there would be no more degrading appointments like this.

The elevator doors slid open with barely a whisper. There were no buttons inside, just a camera. I turned my eyes toward the black orb in the ceiling until the doors closed and began to descend. The highly polished metal provided me a warped reflection of myself. I ran a hand through my hair then straightened the cuffs on my shirt to try to conceal my annoyance.

Gentle piano music greeted me as the doors slid open. Plush, sage colored carpet muted my footfalls as I headed toward the door at the end of the hall. I ignored the art and other décor as I'd committed it to memory over the last few months. The original Monet and Renoir had grown stale after the many hours of waiting to see my clan leader.

I didn't bother knocking. She'd know I was here. Instead, I pushed the double doors open and glanced around the room. To the left, a white porcelain tea set waited in the sitting area. The back wall held a huge flat screen TV. Two burly men with unblinking, golden eyes stood at attention next to a second set of double doors, which I ignored. My focus landed on the fragile looking girl as she played the white grand piano dominating the right side of the room.

Her waist-length hair was so pale it glowed white under the overhead lights. Every movement was precise, every note perfect. She was dressed in a knee length red lace dress with a modest neckline and flowing sleeves. Her long fingers were tipped with nails painted the exact shade of the dress.

As the last note faded, she turned and bestowed me a beaming smile. Someone on the street would estimate her age to be between nine and eleven. However, it was anyone's guess how old she actually was. I'd seen what happened to the last person who had asked and I was not about to repeat their mistake.

"Victor," her voice had a singsong quality, accentuated with the slight French lilt. "What an unexpected surprise."

"Seraphine, a pleasure as always." I bowed my head in greeting.

She skipped over and settled herself on the settee across from the tea. Considering the tea was waiting to be poured, I doubted very much my visit was a surprise. I had obviously been the last to know about my forced sabbatical.

Taking a deep calming breath, I lowered myself into the chair next to Seraphine and poured the tea. She took two sugars; I took none. After she had taken a sip and let out a contented sigh, I knew I could speak my peace.

"I am formally requesting temporary relocation."

"Oh?" Seraphine took another sip and looked innocently over her cup at me.

She was going to make me spell it out. "My firm has requested I take a leave of absence. I have agreed and would like… I mean, I am requesting permission to relocate to Montana so I may spend time with my sister. Her calming effect would do me some good."

Seraphine nodded toward the plate of shortbread cookies. I retrieved the plate and offered the desserts to her. She mused over them for a moment then picked one at random. Her tiny mouth savored each crumb before responding to my request.

"Your choice of location has nothing to do with unfinished business?" Her brilliant blue eyes locked with mine and I knew I couldn't lie.

"Yes, and no. I made the mistake of binding myself to…" my jaw clenched and I was unable to speak her name, "that woman. But now that I am reborn, as well as immortal, it holds little meaning. I am still adjusting to the change and think time away would speed my transition as well as come to terms with my situation."

"I have never been to Montana. Is it nice?" Seraphine asked casually.

"It depends on your definition. There are more cattle than people. It gets extremely cold in the winter but holds some of the most beautiful sights known to man."

Seraphine smiled knowingly. "I'm sure it does. Your request has been granted."

"Thank-" I began.

She slammed her teacup down, shattering the delicate cup and saucer. "I wasn't finished! Your request has been granted. However, you are to continue regular check-ins and if I find out you lied to me as to why you have chosen such a place to relocate… Well, I don't really need to tell you what happens then, do I?"

"No explanation necessary. I plan on staying through New Year's but will keep you apprised of my return date."

Seraphine smiled sweetly as if her outburst and warning never happened. "Now give me a kiss and be on your way. If I eat any more of these cookies, I won't want dinner. I've heard we have quite a variety on the menu tonight. I'd invite you to stay but I'm sure you are anxious to see your sister, was it? Does she possess any wonderful gifts akin to yours?" Seraphine asked as she took the proffered linen napkin from one of the men that had been standing by the doors earlier.

"No, she does not. Unless you consider being unnaturally happy a gift."

The double doors opened, letting in the bass from the dance club above. Half a dozen young women stumbled in accompanied by two more of my clan. Seraphine clapped her hands in delight at the new guests. I nodded a hello to Rowan, another newly reborn member, and the closest thing to a friend I currently had.

"Victor, would you mind?" Seraphine asked.

There was no need for explanation. I'd been a part of Seraphine's bloodbath dinner parties before. It was not something I enjoyed as much as some of the other clan members, but it was an initiation of sorts that could not always be refused. Sometimes, she wanted them to fight; other times, she just wanted to feed.

I made my way to the newcomers, opening my arms with a smile. "Ladies, welcome to the VIP suite."

There was some nervous laughter but they all turned to me as the double doors were closed and bolted. One of the girls in the back clutched her purse and turned nervously toward the way they'd come. The rest watched me with intense curiosity.

I continued and put as much persuasion into my tone as possible. "Seraphine will be your host. Come, take a seat. The real party is about to start."

I gestured first to Seraphine then to the seating area. The tea set was suddenly absent, replaced with a tray of brightly colored shots and champagne chilling on ice. The group slowly edged in that direction, ringed by my clan members.

Once the girls had taken their seats, I made my way toward the exit. The first crash sounded before I made it to the elevator. I suddenly wondered if I'd subdued them all enough that there wouldn't be any screaming, but the face of the tall girl in the back came to mind and I knew there would most definitely be screaming.

It had taken all my willpower to keep my anger in check. Had I known Seraphine only agreed to grant my immortality status contingent upon my power of persuasion, I may have reconsidered.

As I rode the elevator back to the parking garage, I knew that was a lie. As soon as I'd found out immortality was an option, I'd sought her out and began the process. I didn't want to die but now wasn't sure if this was how I wanted to live either.

* * *

My doorbell rang at exactly eight PM. Deborah was apparently punctual after hours as well. I'd prepared a rack of lamb, rosemary spiced red potatoes, and white asparagus for dinner. Not that I would be enjoying any of it. Since my transition, my diet was strictly liquid. Only living immortals like Seraphine could enjoy the little things like those damned shortbread cookies. I missed cooking. I missed food.

"Good evening," I said as I opened the door, unable to hold back a smirk at my own bad vampire joke.

Deborah wore quite a bit more makeup than she did at the office. Her newly highlighted hair was pulled up in a trendy style with loose curls here and there. Long silver earrings dripped from her ears to her shoulders, providing easy access to her neck. Her smile seemed a bit unsure as I stepped back and motioned for her to enter.

I relieved her of the wine bottle then helped her out of her long white coat. She murmured a thank you and stepped into the dining room. I stored her coat out of the way and offered her my arm as I headed back to the kitchen. Try as she might, her nervousness bled through her forced nonchalant attitude.

"You have a beautiful home," Deborah said as I handed her a glass of wine.

"Thank you. You look quite beautiful yourself."

A faint blush rose to her cheeks and she looked through her false lashes at me in what I'm sure she believed was an alluring manner. She'd really gone all out for this evening. The black, form fitting cocktail dress was so new it still smelled of the store, as well as the last three people who tried it on. Even her acrylic nails had been touched up since I'd seen her two days ago. The way she shifted her weight to the left suggested the silver heels hadn't been broken in yet either.

"Shall we?" I motioned toward the already set table.

I served us both then watched as Deborah picked at her food, taking only one bite of everything. Women like her subsisted on celery and air. Those three bites were probably more calories than everything else she'd eaten all day. The silence was welcoming to me but I could tell it made Deborah even more nervous.

"I'll miss seeing your smiling face while I'm away."

Deborah poorly hid her giddy response with a sip of wine. The wine was awful. Probably less than fifteen bucks at the grocery store but I drank it anyway and every now and then picked up my fork. My ruse didn't fool her.

"Seems like neither one of us is very hungry tonight."

"Would you like a tour of the rest of the house?" I offered.

She nodded so I hurried around the table to pull out her chair. She'd finished two glasses of the horrid wine and wobbled a bit on her way up. I wrapped her arm around mine and steadied her without her even noticing. Even with her heels, the top of her head barely reached my shoulder.

I'd purposely left the lights off in the living room and turned on the patio ones. I guided her on the step down into the living room and let her set the pace to the huge window and sliding glass door that overlooked the city.

"Wow. I bet the sunsets are amazing here."

I inwardly sighed. Yet another thing I had taken for granted and now missed.

"Oh! And you have a pool." She seemed positively delighted.

"Closed for the winter I'm afraid," I half joked as I gently guided her toward the back of the house.

The pool had been drained after my unfortunate accident and I couldn't bring myself to look at it without losing control of my tenuous calm. Deborah squirmed slightly and I loosened my grip on her arm as I showed her the rest of the house, saving the master suite for last.

If I was heading north tomorrow, I was going to need to be sated both physically and well… physically. The California king bed dominated the center of the room. Black pillar candles flickered around the periphery. I let loose of Deborah's arm and took her by the hand. She gave no resistance when I moved us closer to the bed. I had never forced a woman in my mortal life and I wasn't about to start in my immortal one.

Deborah melted into my kiss then giggled when I lifted and carried her to the bed. She lay back with her arms above her head and stared at me with partially glazed eyes. I kissed from her knees down to her ankle and gently removed first one shoe then the next. My hands skimmed her perfectly smooth legs all the way up under her dress to her waist; she wasn't wearing any panties. I grabbed her hips and pulled her to the edge of the bed and buried my face between her legs. She bucked and moaned appreciatively.

After a shuddering orgasm, I moved upward, removing the remainder of her clothing followed quickly by my own. I started out gentle but lost myself in the moment. It had been too long. The last time had been with… *her*.

"Ouch, Victor." Deborah gasped. "You're hurting me."

The memory of it played behind my eyelids and I ignored Deborah's cries. After all this time, she shouldn't still hold so much power over me. I had survived and become stronger. How could she still torment me so?

"Stop. Victor, please stop." Deborah pushed weakly against my chest.

"You want the pain to stop, Arabella?" I whispered harshly in her ear.

"What? Yes, please make it stop." Deborah sobbed.

"Your pain ends when mine does."

As I climaxed, I grabbed her hair and yanked her head to the side. Another gasp of pain escaped her lips before my teeth sunk into her neck. Rich, wine tainted blood poured down my dry throat and I pulled hard. Deborah's cries of pain returned once again to moans of ecstasy as I drank more and more. Her heart began to flutter and her arm fell from my shoulder. As I drained the last of her, I heard her spine snap against my hold.

Disgusted, I pushed her limp body off the end of the bed. I'd call the clan tomorrow before I departed to deal with the body. I'd still write the letter of support for Deborah and submit it to my boss. It was a shame. She really was a damn good secretary.

Chapter Three

In the past, I've been described as impatient and intolerant of those beneath me. A rage now smoldered just below the surface, barely under my control. I lashed out at everyone sometimes with words, other times with physical violence of which I'd never before dreamed I was capable. Blood helped but it didn't extinguish the fire.

"For your safety and comfort, we ask that you please remain seated with your seatbelt securely fastened until the captain turns off the Fasten Seat Belt sign. Check the area around your seat for any personal belongings you may have brought onboard with you and please use caution when opening the overhead bins, as heavy articles may have shifted during the flight. American Regional Airlines thanks you for choosing us for your travel needs and we look forward to seeing you again in the near future."

Focusing on the flight attendant's high-pitched whine was the only thing that kept me from ripping the throat out of the man sitting next to me. He'd never stopped eating or talking during the entire flight. It felt like my right side was covered in his greasy saliva from the way he sprayed when he pronounced certain words.

"It was great to meet you, Vincent," Hungry Man stated then offered his hand.

"Victor," I corrected him and pointedly ignored his greasy mitt.

He was not deterred. His sweaty palm pounded my back in a juvenile display of approval. I stared at the hideously orange hair of the woman in front of me and prayed for the seatbelt sign to go out. Even in first class, I was surrounded by people unworthy of sharing my air.

In truth, the recycled air was giving me a headache. The stench of sweat, cologne, food, and idiocy were overpowering. The stout man seated across the aisle smelled so strongly of vodka that I was sure he had more alcohol than blood in his system. I'd watched the man play grab-ass with the entire flight staff, even the men.

The second the seatbelt light flashed, I was up and opening the overhead bin containing my carry-on bag. I'd made it halfway up the aisle before a behemoth of a woman stepped out in front of me. I glanced around her toward the flight attendant standing by the open door. She gave me an understanding look and shrugged. I sighed and tried to calm myself for the wait.

"Victor!" Eve bounced and waved as I walked through the arrivals gate.

As I shifted my carry-on, a squat, balding man shoved past as he hurried toward baggage claim. He reeked of cheap liquor and body odor. To my right, a mother hurried along twin girls complete with blonde pigtails. A group of dander-headed frat boys laughed and joked about which bars had the hottest chicks. Behind them, an elderly couple shuffled hand in hand as if they had no destination in mind at all.

Sheep. They were all fucking sheep. Come to think of it, that is an insult to sheep. At least animals could sense danger. I had to get away before I slaughtered every last one. I could take out the closest ten before anyone even realized a predator was in their midst. Idiotic, over populating, space wasting maggots.

"Victor?" Eve waved her hand in front of my face.

I quickly rearranged my features and focused on my baby sister. She smelled like fabric softener and pomegranates. Her pink angora sweatsuit and ski jacket made her look like a life-size Barbie, complete with blonde hair again. Her smile radiated such love I had to smile myself. An action that felt odd after so long.

"It's so cold here. Did you bring a better coat?" Eve asked.

"You worry too much." I wrapped my arm around her shoulder and kissed the top of her head. "Let's get my bag and get out of here. Can't wait to check out your new place."

Eve began to prattle on about her condo and her first semester at the local university. My eyes darted from face to face, lingering on none. So unaware, so fragile, yet they served a purpose. The fat man who bumped into me earlier struggled to lift his bag from the luggage carousel. It held a tag with his address. I made a mental note of it. He and I would have a little chat about manners over dinner soon.

Eve's BMW navigated the icy roads with ease. She had the heater cranked as high as it would go yet was still hunched up and shivering. A California girl through and through. I still couldn't figure out why she had chosen Montana for college. Actually, I could. Her relationship with our mother was never what one would call amicable. Then there was Eve's off-again on-again relationship with Acacia, not to mention how close she'd gotten to…

"Here we are!" Eve started bouncing again as we drove down a small decline.

Her silver SUV pulled smoothly into the covered parking space at the new condo complex right next to the river. The leaf-bare trees held a layer of frost that glowed in the moonlight. As I stepped out of the car, the night air glittered with ice crystals. Eve's breath puffed out as white as she hurried to her front door. I huffed a laugh. She looked like a pink cotton ball scurrying across the icy walkway.

By the time I managed to wrangle both my bags to her door, Eve had neatly hung up her coat and set her boots on a mat just inside the door. A cute hand painted sign read, "Please take off your shoes. The hardwood floors thank you".

"Your room is straight ahead all the way back," Eve called from upstairs. "I'm making us some tea."

Her voice sounded muffled and far away as I took a deep breath. I knew I'd have to face my past but I hadn't expected to be assaulted with it the second I walked through Eve's front door. I staggered and reached toward the wall for support.

Her scent hung thickly in the air, as if she were standing right in front of me. Eve must have had her over earlier today. I could picture every detail: guarded golden eyes, the perfect waves of caramel colored hair, the sweetness of her skin, her smoky laughter, and snarky wit. Everything that made me love her, and everything that made me hate her.

The handle of my luggage cracked under my grip. I wasn't safe. I needed to get away from Eve, away from the memory of the woman who tormented me every second since I first laid eyes on her.

"Eve, can I borrow your car?" I struggled to keep my voice casual.

The clanging around in the kitchen stopped. In the silence that followed, I imagined my sweet sister chewing her thumbnail and shifting her weight from foot to foot as she considered her answer.

"Did you forget something? I can pick up anything you need tomorrow while you sleep," she offered, still not moving from her spot in the kitchen.

"I'm just worked up from the flight. Driving calms my nerves."

Eve appeared at the top of the stairs, her warring emotions clear on her face. She wanted to let me take the car but she didn't want me to seek out and possibly harm her friend. Her large brown eyes searched mine for signs that I might be out for revenge.

"Eve, hon, I've never been good at sitting still. I promise just a quick spin and I'll be back." I hated to do it but I let my power of persuasion slip into my words.

Eve gave me a half smile and nodded. “The keys are hanging by the door. Make sure you park in spot 21. If you go by the Supermart, grab some ice cream?”

“I thought you were cold.” I laughed.

“It’s never too cold for ice cream,” Eve said as I closed the door behind me.

Chapter Four

Driving had always been my relaxant of choice when I was mortal. Luckily, it was one of the things that stayed through my transition. One of the many perks of being immortal meant I could drive faster and more reckless. I'd already destroyed two Ferraris, a Jaguar, and my Aston Martin causing no permanent damage to myself with the exception of a ripped suit jacket in one case.

Snow-covered trees flew past my window as I accelerated around another bend. It had taken an extreme amount of restraint not to drive straight to my tormentor's house. Instead, I drove south, out of town, then west up into the wooded mountains. I hadn't passed another vehicle so I'd been using both lanes as I drove well above the posted limit. The faster I went, the clearer my mind became.

As soon as I turned up the two-lane mountain road, I flipped off the headlights and floored it. The all-season tires tried their best to find traction on the ice sheeted curves but failed in most cases. As I spun for the third time and corrected, I was no longer seeing red. My foot relaxed on the accelerator knowing Eve would be devastated if I totaled her car and had to walk back to town. Dad would buy her another without a second thought but I hated upsetting Eve.

My lost memories began to rearrange themselves as the shaking that had racked my body since I stepped into Eve's condo began to subside. It was *her*. It had always been her. The source of my everlasting torment. The reason for my death.

Arabella.

It was time to face my personal purgatory, but how to approach it? Just kill her and take the punishment from my clan? I'd be free then, in a manner of speaking. A century or so of restitution was better than a few decades of being bound to a woman spending her life with my twin brother. Could she ever love me as I loved her? Was there still a chance for the future we were destined to have?

Around the corner stood a herd of deer. The stupid beasts were just standing in the middle of the fucking road! I slammed on the brakes and started to slide. Huge brown eyes watched in paralyzed fear as the SUV hurdled toward it.

The vehicle stopped mere inches from the closest deer. Its white tail flicked a few times then it slowly ambled up the road as if nothing had happened. I watched until the herd disappeared then I turned the SUV around and headed back to town.

Instead of heading straight back to Eve's, I opened the browser on my phone and looked up the Supermart. It was a twenty-four-hour place where the night shifters went before heading home and the ultra-weird hung out because nothing else was open. Two dozen or so vehicles dotted the enormous parking lot, all of which had parked wherever they felt like stopping. There was snow on the ground so parking in a designated spot or even straight was obviously no longer required.

I grabbed a bright blue shopping basket and hung it in the crook of my arm. The produce section accosted me with the scent of overly ripe and rotten fruit. A greasy looking teen was pushing a broom between the displays, appearing more like a zombie than an employee. Ahead were two women dressed in ripped fishnets and dresses at least two sizes too small, complete with enough makeup to make them somewhat attractive in low light. Unfortunately, this was not the case in the harsh fluorescence of the Supermart.

Luckily, the frozen section was between the hookers and me. I turned and glanced at the hundreds of flavors, sizes, and brands. For the life of me, I could not remember what kind Eve preferred. I opened a door at random and reached in. The shaking began again as I took in the label. Caramel Swirl. Arabella's favorite.

The tub bulged and compressed as my grip tightened. The lid popped off and ice cream started to run onto the floor in large globs. The zombie pushing the broom rounded the corner at that moment.

"Hey! You're gonna have to pay for that, asshole!" he yelled.

I dropped the mess on the floor and slowly turned to face him. The smile that crossed my face was one of the few genuine ones I'd felt since my transition. The zombie boy paled even further then held his hands up in submission, broom handle smacking against the floor like a gunshot. The basket dropped from my arm as I took a step in his direction.

"Fuck you, Rodge," a woman's voice spoke from behind me. "It's your job to clean up this dump."

One of the prostitutes I'd seen earlier slipped her arm around my waist and snuggled close. The scent of cheap perfume, hair spray, and stale cigarettes rose up as her jacket pressed against my side. Instead of pushing her away, I snaked my arm around her shoulders, careful not to dig my fingers into her soft flesh.

"You lookin' for a good time, tall, dark and handsome?" she asked, smacking her gum.

"Only if it involves your friend too," I answered, softening my smile for her.

She popped her gum in delight then turned us the way she had come. "Georgia, come on, girl. We're too good for this place."

"Holy shit, it's cold out here," Georgia complained as we stepped outside.

"Where's your car, handsome?" the hooker on my arm asked as she snuggled closer.

I reached out my other arm toward Georgia and she gratefully pressed her body against mine hoping for warmth. Too bad there was none to share. We rounded the corner and my grin deepened. A truck complete with a pop-up camping trailer was parked under a tree that bordered the vacant lot behind the Supermart.

"Why'd ya park so far away?" Georgia grumbled.

"You don't look like the kinda fella who drives something like that," the nameless hooker commented.

I chuckled under my breath. "Looks can be deceiving, ladies."

"And money talks," Georgia retorted, slowing her steps slightly.

I unwound my arm from Nameless and flipped open my wallet. "Two hundred for each of you now and depending on how it goes, there is another two hundred after."

As I suspected, Georgia grabbed all the cash and began hurrying toward the truck. My enhanced eyesight and hearing told me both the truck and camper were empty, most likely abandoned for some time. I reached around and easily broke the lock, then opened the door for the hookers to go in ahead of me.

"Where's the light?" Georgia asked as she bumped into something that smashed to the floor.

"I don't need light," I whispered, as I could see them as if it were midday.

"Cool. Your eyes look like a cat's. Look, G, they glow."

Georgia didn't look impressed, more like she was ready to bolt. I positioned myself between her and the door then reached for Nameless. Steeling myself for the drug and disease-ridden blood, I first pressed my lips to her ear and moved down her throat. A barely audible whimper escaped when my fangs pierced her jugular, and I began to drink. Her blood was tainted with some sort of opiate but otherwise she was disease free. Not that it mattered, I was immune to anything this filth might carry.

“What about me, mister.” Georgia moved closer and petted Nameless’s hair, unaware her friend was close to cardiac arrest due to blood loss.

I dropped the first hooker and she crashed to the floor.

“What the fuck?” Georgia bent to check on her but I grabbed her hair and yanked her farther into the trailer.

Her scream was cut short when I backhanded her, nose and jaw crunching with the blow. One of her teeth hit the wall as I now dragged her limp body to the back. I had two hours until sunrise, plenty of time for both my pleasure and her pain.

Chapter Five

I did allow myself a few minutes to drive by Arabella's place before heading back to Eve's. The cottage style house was just as quaint as I remembered, only now surrounded by drifts of carefully shoveled snow. Her blue Mustang sat in the drive and frost covered the windows, leading me to believe she'd been home for hours. All the windows were dark. I closed my eyes and pictured her lying in her bed, one leg outside the blankets and hair spilling across both pillows. Clothes would be strewn around her room but her kitchen would be spotless. I could almost smell the popcorn and cocoa she would have enjoyed before bed.

My fingers twitched toward my phone resting in the cup holder. I suddenly longed to hear her voice again. After struggling to enter the passcode, I stared at her name on my contacts list. My thumb hovered over the call icon for a full minute before I threw the phone into the footwell of the passenger seat and floored it.

Killing her was never really an option. As much as I loathed the power she held over me, I loved her. I needed her. Even being this close to her seemed to provide a calm that I'd been searching for since my rebirth. I'd been foolish to leave the decision up to her before. She was mine. She'd always been mine. No fucking around this time. It would take time but she too would realize she belonged with, and to, me.

As I approached the main streets, I slowed and tried to calm my frantic mind. I needed a plan to get around Arabella's infatuation with my brother, her misguided hatred toward me, and that pesky restraining order.

Through my recovery and beyond, my family hadn't mentioned her name or the events leading up to my "death". It had been my father's whisperings that gave me my greatest idea. He'd been with Eve visiting me shortly after my rebirth, before I'd even been released from the recovery facility. Everyone still believed I was sleeping.

"What do we tell Victor about Arabella and Tom?" Eve asked.

"Will he even remember?" Lucien asked.

"How could he not remember?" Eve's voice rose above a whisper for a second.

"The transformation affects everyone differently. Maybe he doesn't remember all the details," Lucien suggested then added, "For everyone's sake, I hope he doesn't."

From that point on, I'd shown no emotion when Tom or Tom's fiancée had been brought up. My family was very careful to not use her first name for fear it would trip my recognition and I would go all vengeful and tarnish our family's good name. Hell, I'd even convinced Tom that he and I were well on our way to a fragile friendship. Obviously, I'd gotten all the brainpower when we shared the womb. Seraphine, however, was not fooled. She saw all the rage and desperation I'd kept buried around everyone else.

The amnesia angle could work but Arabella would be suspicious. It wasn't a complete lie either; holes still plagued my memory. The holidays were the perfect excuse to slowly push my way back into her life. Eve would have warned her of my visit so running into her was another option. Well, a hundred feet from her was an option, as I did not have time to sit in a jail cell for ignoring the restraining order. Christmas dinner should be a good enough excuse for a little forced proximity.

The sky had just begun to lighten as I parked Eve's SUV in spot 21. The sun wouldn't be over the mountains for some time yet so I headed toward the river. Ice clung to the banks but the river still flowed freely. I watched as the sky lightened from slate gray to lavender complete with wispy yellow clouds. This was the closest thing to a real sunrise I'd ever see again.

Reluctantly, I shut myself in Eve's condo. The lower level was pitch dark but I could almost feel the sun starting to peek into the upstairs windows. Its affect caused a physical fatigue that slid over my entire body almost to the point of pain. Eve's slow, level breathing sounded from the top of the stairs.

Another genuine smile touched my lips. She'd fallen asleep on the couch waiting for me. Too bad I'd not gotten her ice cream, not that I'd be able to put it in the kitchen upstairs at this point anyway.

My suitcase was not where I'd left it just inside the door. I quietly removed my shoes and made my way to the back bedroom where I found all my bags. The windows had been light blocked, professionally by the looks of it. The bed was turned down and a glass of water sat on the nightstand. Even a phone charger was plugged in and waiting. My little sis would be an amazing mother someday.

I found a small bathroom across the hall. The weight of the sun was making me stumble but I needed a shower. The stench of death clung to me, as did the stale air from the plane.

Tomorrow I would start my new life. I was done with being told what to do and being led around like a disobedient toddler. I'd chosen to be immortal and I would live my very long life by my own design.

* * *

The front door bumped quietly closed and I opened my eyes. Admitting I hadn't heard Eve leave this morning filled me with mixed emotions. First was dread that I'd been so out of it then acceptance that I felt safe enough here to sleep that deeply.

I waited a few minutes so Eve didn't think she'd woken me up before I rolled out of bed. I wanted to take her to dinner; to start showing her how much she meant to me. I'd been selfish and it was time to make amends.

Eve puttered around somewhat quietly, humming to herself as I ascended the stairs. Her living room was modestly furnished with a loveseat and the largest beanbag chair I'd ever seen. A huge abstract painting dominated the main wall and a large flat screen hung above the fireplace. Everything was black and white with accent splashes of primary colors which complemented the pale wood flooring.

"Oh, you're up," Eve said, finally noticing me. "I didn't hear you come in last night."

The unanswered question hung between us. "I drove up the pass, watched the sunrise, then slept like the dead."

My joke took a second to sink in but Eve laughed, really laughed, and so did I.

"What would you like for dinner?" Eve asked, opening the fridge then shutting it slowly. "Oh, sorry."

"Don't apologize. I'd love to treat my baby sister to dinner. What are you in the mood for?"

"There's a great pizza place that actually has pretty good wine."

"Done," I answered. "Let me get dressed and we'll go."

I recognized the pizza place as the one Arabella had attempted to take me to that summer only to find it was booked out. Tonight, there were people coming and going so it was clearly open for business. With a town this small, I had a feeling I'd be running into more and more memories that involved her.

"I'll get us a table if you want to wait outside." Eve's offer sounded almost like a question.

"People won't bother me tonight. It's just me and you, kid."

She smiled and let me open the door for her. The place was loud and bright. I did a scan but heard her laugh before I spotted them. Tom and Arabella were sitting with their backs to the door. Cassie glanced my way for a second then went back to her conversation without showing any sign of recognition. She was sitting very close to a tall Native American man.

"This way." The hostess grabbed two menus and started in the direction of Arabella's table.

Eve got half a dozen steps then froze once Arabella and Tom's backs came into view. "Actually, can we sit at the bar?"

"Of course." The hostess turned sharply away from the table and we followed her to the bar that ran along one wall. We were out of sight of the table but close enough I could hear every word.

"Bottle of Shiraz," I said as the bartender approached us.

"Lemonade, please," Eve added then turned to face me. "Are you okay, or should we go someplace else?"

"I'm fine. This is where you wanted to go so this is where we shall stay." Eve looked worried and curled her menu in thought, so I added in a lower voice, "I promise not to make a scene. Maybe they won't even see us. Tell me more about this Art History class you both love and hate so much."

She took the bait and began to chatter on about how much she loved the teacher but how boring the content was. I nodded and added responses as necessary but I was focused on the conversation at another table.

"I heard you finally found a dress," Cassie gushed. "I can't believe your wedding dress is red but I wouldn't expect anything traditional for you, Arabella."

"The dress found me. Who was I to say no?"

"I'm surprised you're having a big ceremony. I imagined a date with the justice of the peace and a barbeque reception afterward," Cassie continued.

Tom cut in, "January is not exactly barbeque weather."

Cassie scoffed. "In Montana, any month is barbeque weather. It's not that I'm complaining or anything. My Arabella just isn't your normal bride."

"Let's talk about something else." Arabella nearly pleaded. "Stan, I know you probably hate talking about medical stuff outside of work, but I had a question about the flu that's going around."

"You don't feel sick, do you?" Tom asked.

"No, and I already got my flu shot. It's you I'm worried about. You'll be working crazy hours and spending more time on the tour bus than I like to think about, not to mention all those fans that wouldn't dream of staying home from your concert because they're feeling under the weather."

Stan replied, "My clinic still has vaccines available and walk-ins are Wednesday and Friday from eleven to six."

Tom answered. "I'm not a fan of needles. Plus, I've never had the flu or a flu shot. Why ruin a perfect record?"

Stan let out his breath. "You seem healthy enough and you aren't in the high-risk group so the choice is up to you. If you do get the flu, you'll probably only be down for a day or two. Besides, if you've never had a flu shot, you might have a mild reaction."

"Who's in the high-risk group?" Cassie asked.

"Normally, senior citizens, infants under six months, and anyone with a history of respiratory illness are first in line for vaccinations." Stan paused. "The CDC just sent out new guidelines at the end of this week. According to new studies, young adults and middle-aged people with the vampirion *gene are more susceptible to life threatening complications. From what I've seen at the clinic, I'm inclined to agree. I've never seen the flu season hit so hard so early."*

Eve was waving her hand in front of my face. "Hello, did you hear me?"

I blinked and focused on my sister. "I'm sorry. My brain shuts off sometimes. What did you say?"

"I asked if you wanted me to cancel my Christmas dinner party so it could just be you and me?"

"Why would I want that?"

Eve lifted her thumb toward her mouth then frowned at the bad habit. "Acacia, Tom, and Arabella were invited and I didn't know…"

"I'm sorry I dropped in on you so unexpectedly. My firm is forcing an extended leave of absence and I couldn't bear to sit alone in my house for who knows how long, especially over the holidays."

Her expression softened upon hearing my explanation so I continued. "Eve, I want you to do what is important to you. You've had a lot of expectations set on your shoulders. I think it's time you stood on your own, made some of your own decisions."

Eve launched herself out of her chair and hugged me. "Thank you. You have no idea how much that means to me."

"Eve? Victor?"

Eve jerked away. I closed my eyes and took a deep breath before turning to the voice. "Hey, baby bro. How's it going?"

Tom pulled me in for a hug. "It's good, really good. I had no idea you were in town. What's the occasion?"

There was no accusation in his tone. He fully believed our relationship was mending. "Holidays, and I had some vacation time saved up at work."

"It's good to see you, man. Are you staying at Eve's? Maybe I can swing by and we can catch up."

Eve smothered Tom in a hug and answered for me. "Yeah, he's staying in my awesome condo. Jealous much?"

I could tell Eve was trying to ease any tension with humor but it clearly wasn't necessary. Tom slapped me on the back and studied me for a few seconds. He snuck a glance toward the table where his party had been sitting to find it empty.

"You really do look good, man. I've gotta run but I'll do my best to stop by."

"Don't worry about it. I'm sure you're busy with all the wedding plans." My voice caught a bit on the last two words and a heavy silence hung in the air.

"Uh, something like that. If I don't get a chance, I'll see you on Christmas. We're still on for dinner, right, Eve?"

Chapter Six

It was stupid and risky but I found myself following Arabella during her late night jobs. Spending time with her, even at a distance, helped calm me somehow, like the constant itch under my skin eased. She'd gotten better at surveying space and crowds but it didn't matter, I was too good to be caught. Her confidence was clear, as was her increased reaction time, but I was up for the challenge.

Tonight, for example, Geo had assigned her as an escort slash protection for a city councilman. Apparently, his newest bill had angered some local gun activists leading to why he needed protection in the first place. The event was a swanky benefit dinner for a local non-profit organization. At three hundred fifty per plate, it was a shame I could only drink wine but the view wasn't bad.

This was a black-tie affair and Arabella had been forced to dress for the occasion. The dark blue backless dress looked like something my sister picked out. Her hair was up in a fancy twist, exposing her neck in a very luxurious way. Everything about her looked better, healthier. A tiny silver cross glittered at the base of her throat.

"You know, you wouldn't look too bad if you invested in some contacts and a push-up bra," the asshole client whispered a little too loudly to her.

Arabella's expression flashed from hurt to angry then back to indifferent professional. If she only knew how she wore her expressions so clearly.

She was absolutely gorgeous. How dare he make her doubt herself. I clenched my teeth and fought the urge to rip his head off.

"Get me another drink, Angela," the asshole commanded.

"It's Arabella," she said flatly. "And I don't leave your side."

It would have been entertaining to see her struggle to keep the drunk upright but he was getting a bit too grabby for her- and my- liking. The wineglass stem snapped against my grip when he squeezed her ass hard enough to make her jump.

“Thank you for the donation, Victor. Will you still be in town this summer to see your contribution at work?”

I’d been chatting with one of the women who ran the non-profit while I watched my prize. She was in her early fifties and not unattractive. Rings sparkled on every finger except the third finger on her left hand. The way she leaned in and played with her hair told me she was trying to flirt, for more money or something else I wasn’t sure.

Arabella agilely diverted her client toward the bar for another drink. The asshole attempted to hit on the bartender as Arabella continued to scan the room. Her gaze skipped over where I had been standing moments ago. It was childish but I’d bent down to pretend to tie my shoe. When I straightened, she was leading her client toward the exit.

“I’d love to relocate to the area but there are some logistical issues. If you would please excuse me.” The woman opened her mouth to protest so I let persuasion sink into my next words, "I'll be right back."

Her smile seemed a bit forced but my words worked. I touched her arm in farewell and a blush rose to her cheeks. Without another word, I turned and followed Arabella out of the building.

She got into a nondescript dark colored sedan after depositing her client in the passenger seat. I waited until they were on the street before following. They only made it to the first light before he opened the door and vomited. The seatbelt seemed to be the only thing keeping him in the vehicle. Arabella pulled rolling stops for the remainder of the trip, clearly trying to get him home as quickly as possible.

When she pulled up a private lane, I continued past not wanting to rouse suspicion. I parked around the bend and hurried through the trees toward the house. My shoes were not fit for the snowy hillside and would most likely have to be replaced.

"Finally," Arabella muttered after attempting the alarm code three times. She pushed the door open then mostly carried her client inside the house.

I listened as she deposited her charge before clearing the house room by room. Lights flipped on and off to show her progress. She struggled to close an open window but it was followed by the sound of running water, and a short shriek. It took all my willpower to keep from bolting from my hiding spot.

"Don't sneak up on me like that, kitty-kitty. You'll take care of him after I leave, right?" Arabella cooed, followed by the loudest purr I've ever heard.

"Thanks for choosing Geo's Security for your protection needs," she deadpanned to the snoring man as she backed out the front door. God, I missed her sarcasm.

I watched as she wrapped her arms around herself against the cold and hurried to her car. The long dress and slick driveway slowed her progress. The red light of her client's security system blinked on when she moved into its view.

"I hate dresses," she mumbled under her breath as she slid into the driver's seat.

The thunk of her heels getting tossed into the passenger seat was no surprise. She probably had a pair of fuzzy boots waiting for her. Blue light filled the cab as she checked her phone.

The car roared to life, headlights cutting a path to where I was crouched. Luckily, I could hear the radio stations flipping so I knew she wasn't looking in my direction. Slowly, I slid back into the darkness. The first few bass notes from one of my favorite songs thumped before she slowly descended the private lane.

Making note of the cameras, I moved slowly toward the house. The security system was the same as mine so I recognized the sound of the alarm code, and the handle lock on the door was easy enough to break with a sharp twist. The house was quiet except for the hum of the appliances and the man's snoring.

"Mer-ow?" the cat had come up and was rubbing against my leg.

Carefully, I pushed it away until it scurried off. The man was lying face down on a chaise lounge just inside the main door. The smell of urine told me he was passed out hard. What a waste of space.

Arabella's time was better spent than with this worthless piece of garbage. If she was with me, she wouldn't have to degrade herself protecting bastards like this. He had hurt her emotionally and physically tonight. That was not something I was going to allow.

I rolled the man onto the floor with my foot. He bounced slightly but his snoring didn't even slow. Arabella's hurt expression flitted through my memory and I realized I could do something good with my immorality. I needed to feed and assholes like this needed to die.

The cat hissed when I sunk my teeth into the man's neck. Based on the taste of his blood alone, there was a good chance he was well on his way to alcohol poisoning. No one was going to miss this meat sack. And more importantly, he would never hurt my Arabella again.

The cat sniffed its dead owner once I'd finished.

"Don't worry, little one. I'll make sure to fill your bowl before I leave.

* * *

Three days later, the itch under my skin continued to grow no matter what I used to distract myself. Eve had gone to sleep about an hour ago and I was climbing the walls. After flipping through her four hundred channels for the third time, I put on my shoes and a jacket then headed toward the river trail. Maybe I could find a bite to eat. My mouth twitched into a grin at the unintentional pun.

The river trail went under two bridges before entering the park. The normal homeless camps were absent, most likely due to the cold. That wasn't my preferred option for blood but it would work in a pinch. There were half a dozen bars just off the trail so I wouldn't have to work too hard to find a willing donor.

Upon nearing the pavilion, I noticed an event in full swing. The covered area was surrounded with tall patio heaters and was packed with people celebrating. A large table of food, complete with tiered cake, stood in the center. Music played from portable speakers, giving the small gathering some ambiance. Conversation and laughter pulled me toward the crowd. Company was not really what I was seeking tonight so I looked for a place to observe.

The streetlamp that normally illuminated a group of park benches was dark. Taking advantage of the shadows, I sat and watched the party for a time. The itch significantly lessened for the moment, letting my mind calm.

Tiny snow crystals floated in the air. They were not quite snowflakes, as it was too cold, but beautiful just the same. I was about to continue along the path when a voice caught my attention and I tilted my head toward the building that I assumed held the restrooms so I could hear better.

"It's all bullshit, Cassie." Arabella's annoyance was clear.

"What is?"

She sighed before continuing. "Whatever act Victor is putting on to charm my family. I don't understand how everyone can just forgive and forget. The man is a monster."

"Have you seen him yet?" Cassie asked.

"No, and if I had my way, I would never see him again," Arabella said. "But I rarely get my way these days so I'll be seeing him at Christmas dinner at Eve's."

"What about the restraining order?"

Another sigh. "Tom told me to let it go, that his brother has changed. He said Victor has given up his pursuit of me but I just get this feeling… I don't know. Let's just focus on work."

"How about wedding plans? Can we talk about those?"

"No." Her response was flat. "I got to pick out my dress so now I just have to show up. That's all being planned for me as well."

Arabella and Cassie emerged from the small building with two other women, clearly their clients for the night based on their body placement and watchful sweep of the area. Hoping to blend into the shadows, I held still as they quickly made their way back to the party, disappearing into the crowd.

My plan to win her back was deteriorating faster than I could put it in motion. She was too smart for me. Leverage and persuasion wouldn't be enough this time but maybe it didn't have to be. I was under the impression that Arabella and Tom were in pre-matrimonial bliss but that last comment made me wonder.

Against my better judgment, I headed toward the pavilion. Now that I'd seen her, I needed another glimpse. The itch had returned and I only knew one cure. I'd noticed that was the case when I followed her on other jobs.

From listening to various conversations, I was able to surmise this was a birthday party for someone named Ashley. Some were elated for the birthday girl, while others were green with envy. I swiped a glass of champagne and bumped into a lovely dark haired young woman to start up a conversation.

While she flirted with me, I would occasionally scan the crowd for my target. My eyes passed over Cassie twice but I didn't see Arabella again. As she continued to prattle on, I wished I had picked someone with a less irritating voice. She wasn't even worth remembering her name.

"How do you know Ashley?" she asked.

"I work with her cousin," I lied.

The woman laughed. "Weird. I work with her cousin and I've never seen you."

Dropping my gaze to hers, I let a little persuasion sink into my voice. "I'd remember meeting someone as lovely as you."

Her brown eyes widened and she leaned in a bit closer. "Do you want to go someplace a bit more private?"

Sharp fingers bit into my side as a hand snaked around my waist. "Sorry, Sugar, but this one's with me."

I straightened a little before turning my eyes to Cassie. Her smile looked genuine but her gold eyes were downright murderous. After putting my arm around her shoulders, I turned back to the woman I'd been talking to.

"Excuse me. It appears my date needs some attention."

The girl's lower lip protruded in a pout before she turned on her heel and stomped away. Cassie shifted her weight as if to lead us out of the crowd. I followed without any resistance, scrambling to come up with an excuse to be here.

Once we were in the shadows between the party and the restrooms, she shifted her weight again. I thought she was trying to turn to face me but a sharp jab made me look down. She had a handgun pressed against my side.

"How long have you been following Arabella?" Cassie asked, cutting right to the point.

I tried to shift away from her but she shook her head and pressed harder. A shot from that angle wouldn't kill me but it would hurt like hell and I'd have to find blood to undo the damage. Something that was much harder to do when wounded and without the help of my clan.

"I'm not following anyone." I started and she barked a harsh laugh so I continued. "I was bored and hungry so I took a walk. It's a coincidence that we both ended up here. The park is a public space, is it not?"

Cassie's eyes tightened and she stared at me, looking for a lie. Unfortunately for her, everything I said was the truth. Her grip relaxed but she didn't move the gun. After a few moments, she took a step back and put it in the holster.

"Her client had too much to drink so she left. Don't follow her again," Cassie warned. When I opened my mouth to speak, she held up a finger. "She told me everything, Victor. Everything. I'd love to shoot you right now but I am actually still working and you aren't worth the paperwork. If I see you near my friend again, I won't hesitate."

She tapped me between the eyes with her index finger and the threat was received. This woman did not like me and she was looking for any excuse to pull the trigger. Without another word, she turned and walked back to the party.

I let out a breath, not knowing if she'd tell Arabella about this little meeting or not. The annoying young woman I'd been talking to was stalking toward the bathroom. She looked pretty devastated and I realized I needed blood.

Once she exited the building, I pretended to be leaving the men's restroom. She gave me a sad smile and I took the opening.

"Looks like I've flirted with one too many beautiful women. My date left me without a ride home."

The woman looked back at the party for a moment then closed the distance between us. "I'm parked over there."

"Excellent," I said as I put my arm around her.

As we walked away, my steps faltered when I heard Arabella's voice.

"Where'd you go, Cass? You never leave your clients."

Cassie's laugh seemed a bit forced. "Just helping someone who lost their way."

I smiled and picked up my speed. Cassie was a damn good liar and wouldn't worry her friend about our little encounter tonight. I wondered if she realized how much she'd helped me with her vague statement.

Chapter Seven

We were a week away from Christmas and my plans to sway Arabella to me were going absolutely nowhere. According to Eve, she'd requested time off after New Year's, so she was working or sleeping all the time. Bumping into her outside of work wasn't an option anymore and going to her house was a direct violation of that damn restraining order.

The more I watched Arabella at work, the more I noticed the subtle changes. Her caramel hair shone with flecks of red even in the dimmest light, even the gold in her eyes seemed brighter. It appeared she'd lost some weight, which annoyed me, but her curves were still perfectly proportioned. I longed to caress her creamy skin and kiss her lips one more time. Those thoughts consumed me, making me lose focus. Thus, why I was taking a break from following her tonight.

For a change of pace, Eve and I had spent the evening putting the final touches on her Christmas decorations. She'd ordered an artificial blue spruce and ornaments in shades of white, blue, and silver, which matched her new holiday dishes. She wouldn't be my sister without everything perfectly planned and matched. Her living and dining room looked like she'd brought winter inside.

I attached the last of the fairy lights above the fireplace when a knock sounded at the front door.

"Hello, Eve? Are you home?"

Why don't people in Montana lock their doors?

I cursed under my breath. I'd avoided Acacia to this point with school still in session and my sleeping schedule but it couldn't last forever. Besides, I needed her to warm to me if I was to fully gain Arabella's trust.

Eve was in the kitchen listening to Christmas music so I had no buffer when Acacia's head appeared in the living room. She was dressed in black from head to toe. Heavily dark lined eyes narrowed as she focused on me. I feigned indifference as I finished folding up the last decoration box.

I forced a smile. "Acacia. It's nice to see you again."

"Is it though?" she answered, heading to the kitchen with a small white box in her hands.

Eve squealed in delight at whatever Acacia had brought with her. I repressed a sigh as I snapped the storage box closed and headed in their direction. We were approaching zero hour so no time like the present to start swaying the sister.

"I'm so glad you were able to get an early sample. Since I'm making Christmas dinner from scratch, I just didn't think I'd have time to make a dessert too," Eve explained.

"I told you I'd be happy to help in the kitchen." I said, startling both girls.

"Nonsense, you're a guest in my house." Eve grinned. "You can take care of entertaining everyone while I cook."

I felt my smile slip and Acacia bit back a laugh. She turned away from the small dessert then slowly pulled a chef's knife from the butcher block.

"Wanna take a stab at this, Victor?" Acacia asked.

Unconsciously, I adjusted the collar of my shirt and swallowed hard. While my brain had mostly protected me from the moments leading up to my death, the scar and feeling of unease remained. Acacia was going to be a challenge but I was better and had been doing this a lot longer.

"Whatever you need, Eve." I pulled two dessert plates from the cupboard and continued, "I'll be happy to serve you, ladies. As delicious as this looks, I unfortunately will have to pass."

"And why is that?" Acacia asked, checking the tip of the knife with a little too much interest.

"Acacia! Stop it." Eve took the knife from her friend and placed it on the counter near the dessert. "I told you Victor's on a strict diet. Now, let's try this before Tom gets here in case we don't want to share."

The plates clattered together in my hands. "Tom's coming over tonight?"

"Yeah, he's been driving Arabella crazy and she needs to sleep. I'm not sure she's going to be ready for the wedding if she keeps working so much," Eve said then quickly changed the subject as she grabbed her Bluetooth speaker. "We'll take our treat in the living room. I want to show Acacia my new decorations."

I was grateful for their departure. My head was spinning with Acacia's not so veiled threat, my brother's impending visit, and the reminder that the wedding was approaching at breakneck speed.

The thick cheesecake had a dark chocolate crust and was topped with sugared cranberries and edible silver curls that almost floated among the fruit. I cut it evenly into six thin slices then licked my finger without thinking. It was beyond delicious and I hated spitting it back into the sink.

My cell phone rang as I picked up the two filled plates. I put them back down and looked at the screen. Why the fuck would Rowan be calling me?

"What?" I answered.

"Hey, old chap." Rowan's thick British accent was too cheerful for my current mood.

"What do you want?" I repeated.

Rowan cleared his throat before answering. "You've been up north for over two weeks. Not a soul has heard from you."

I closed my eyes and let out a breath. "Well, now you have. I'm at my sister's just like I told Seraphine. I'm hanging up now."

"Wait!" I heard him yell as I pulled the phone away from my ear. "It's too late for that, bruv. I just wanted to let you know I'll be seeing you tomorrow night."

"Hold on a second." I put the phone on the counter and grabbed the plates.

The girls were rearranging the ornaments I had placed on the tree to make them perfect. I would have made a snarky comment but I needed to solve this Rowan problem quickly. The music was much louder in here, which would help cover my conversation in the kitchen.

"I hope it tastes as good as it looks." I handed them each a plate then hurried back to my phone.

"Listen, Rowan," I started in a harsh whisper.

"Boss's orders, Victor. I have no interest in snow but since we're tight, she's sending me. Any good hotels for our kind up there?"

I felt the case on my phone crack as my grip tightened. "I'll call Seraphine now and clear this up."

"I would advise against that. To say she is bloody pissed would be an understatement. I was able to convince her that I could run interference. She wanted to drag you back to California in the noon-day sun."

Fuck. "Fine. Montana's not really equipped for our kind so I'm going to have to make some calls. We'll find you somewhere to stay but you can crash at Eve's when you arrive. Text me your flight info."

I pressed end then jumped when Eve spoke behind me. "Who's staying with us?"

I rearranged my features to appear happy. "A good friend of mine from back home was worried when he hadn't heard from me. The idiot booked a plane ticket before calling. He's got the same sensitivities as I do so I thought maybe he could stay a day or two until we could find him a hotel."

Eve grinned from ear to ear and did a little happy dance. "My first house guest! Besides you, but you're family so it's not really the same. This is a big deal. Acacia!"

Eve skipped back into the living room with the cheesecake box. Obviously, they weren't going to save any for Tom. I followed, trying not to rain on her parade. Rowan would not be staying long and I would not allow my sister to go overboard as hostess on that lecherous old man.

"Victor's friend is coming to stay with us tomorrow." Eve sat down on the beanbag next to Acacia and put the box in the middle so they could share.

"It's not a big deal. I forgot to let Rowan know I was settled and he panicked, thinking I may have done something stupid, or homicidal."

As soon as the words left my mouth, I realized my mistake. Both girls stared at me with wide eyes. I had no idea how much Eve had told Acacia about my rebirth but from her expression, it was enough. This Rowan thing had me off my game.

I let a little persuasion slip into my next words. "He clearly has nothing to worry about. I'm on vacation with my baby sis in snowy Montana. What could possibly go wrong?"

The doorbell rang at that moment. Why did I have to put my big fat foot in my mouth?

"Tom's here." Eve hopped up but stopped long enough to give me a peck on the cheek before meeting out brother at the door.

Acacia sat forward on the beanbag chair while she chewed her bite of cheesecake. "So, you're still a lying piece of shit. Thought maybe death would have helped you chill out but apparently not."

She let the sentence die then looked past me as Eve and Tom got to the top of the stairs. I kept my gaze fixed on the tree. Why hadn't my persuasion had any affect? Did she really hate me to a degree in which I needed to pull out all the stops to have the desired effect?

"Victor!" Tom's voice made me turn and he enveloped me in a hug.

Acacia choked on her cheesecake. "That's something I never thought I'd see."

"Hey Acacia. I didn't see you." Tom reached out to bump her fist but she just looked at him until he awkwardly lowered his hand. "It's all good. Sometimes things have to go to shit to appreciate how important family really is."

Eve put the last sliver of cheesecake on her plate and handed it to Tom. "Here. Tell me what you think. Acacia and I are going to see if we can find any of those holiday cartoons to watch. You boys catch up in the kitchen. We can talk about my new houseguest later."

The look Eve gave me before turning back to Acacia would have made our mother proud. I had no idea someone so cute could also be so scary. The conversation about Rowan was far from over. Maybe I'd leave out the whole British thing. Knowing my luck, she'd buy all new bedding and decorations to make sure his room looked like an

English cottage. Why did girls always go nuts over British guys? Might as well tell her and get it over with or she'd be even more annoyed with me.

"New houseguest?' Tom asked as we headed to the kitchen.

"It's not important." I shook my head. "Bring me up to speed on what's going on with you."

Tom chewed his cheesecake with an appropriate amount of enjoyment before answering. "That is the best cheesecake I've ever eaten. Don't tell my fiancée that or there'll be hell to pay."

He laughed so I joined in. When did this get so hard? We used to be inseparable, almost read each other's minds. Was a blood match really worth losing my twin brother over? Tom's explanation to Acacia made me wonder if he felt the same. Why did one of us always have to lose? And why was it always me?

"My lips are sealed." I mimicked locking my lips and tossing away a key. "I'm glad you stopped by. Sometimes it's tough to really tell how a person feels over the phone or text. I meant it when I said that I was sorry and I missed you. Rebirth has given me perspective and a chance to start over."

"I wish it hadn't gone that far. Immortality is not something I'd wish on my worst enemy," Tom said. "All I want is one normal life with the person I love."

I was thrown by his confession. "Music is a way to live forever. I thought that was your dream."

"It is, in a way. Music lets me tell a story, to share in the triumph and pain of humanity. My dream is to share those emotions with the world. If I'm lucky, maybe my grandkids will hear me on the oldies station and say 'Hey, I love this song. It's a classic'."

Tom's shoulders fell and he placed what was left of the cheesecake on the table before rubbing the back of his neck, an old nervous habit. My expression must have given away my confusion.

"Can't fool you, can I?" Tom laughed nervously then cleared his throat. "Arabella can't have kids. After the accident, I mean."

My throat constricted as I absorbed what he was saying. *The accident.* He meant when I tried to force Arabella to bond with me and she was shot. It wasn't an accident. It was evil. I couldn't win that way. And now I'd taken away something both of us had wanted. God, how could Tom forgive me enough to sit here?

I had to change the subject. "Hey baby bro, I'd give my left nut for a bite of that cheesecake. Immortality isn't all bad but giving up food is a bitch."

Tom chuckled and wiped his cheek with the back of his hand. "Any chance Eve has beer? At least we could share that."

"I'm not twenty-one, you dorks!" Eve called from the living room.

I knew she'd be eavesdropping. Everyone was still on edge about Tom and I patching things up after so long. That and if you looked up worry wart on the internet, you would find a picture of my sister.

"Then how are you constantly restocking my wine?" I called.

There was a brief pause. "Dad?"

Tom and I both cracked up at this. Our sweet sister must have a fake ID. Didn't we all in college? The volume of the TV increased as we continued to laugh. I liked this but it wouldn't last. Losing wasn't an option for me this time. My mistake had already pushed a wedge between Tom and Arabella.

A cough pulled me from my musings. Tom quickly filled a glass with water and downed it.

"This dry air takes some getting used to. If I'm going to have that classic, I'd better start carrying a humidifier around with me. Come on. I'll kick your ass at Spades."

The two of us sat at the table and he indeed kicked my ass. We talked about safe subjects: his music and the progress I'd made on my Mustang. It took me back to college when we would ignore our books and play cards all night. I was never good but Tom was never a sore winner. He always gave me one more chance.

The little fucker had been beating me my entire life! Even in things that didn't matter, like cards. Now that he thought he had won the biggest prize, he was going to sit back and enjoy his spoils. If he thought he'd seen me fight before, he was sorely mistaken. I had nothing but time on my side and this wasn't something I was going to give up on.

The front door crashed open, startling everyone as footsteps thundered up the stairs. My eyes barely registered my assailant before I was getting sucker punched out of the chair. Her fist smashed into my jaw three more times before Tom wrestled her away.

"Nice of you to drop by, Arabella," I said, looking up at her from the floor.

She was shaking with rage, which starkly contrasted her sleep messed hair, giant coat, and fuzzy boots. "You may have everyone else fooled, but I'm *not* an idiot. I won't fall for this shit again. Stay away from my family."

Eve gasped and grabbed Arabella's hand. "You're bleeding."

I licked my lips and the rest of the world fell away. The condo was empty except for me and her. No one nor anything else mattered. While I had been savoring her vanilla and honey scent, the taste of her blood pushed me into nirvana. I was paralyzed in place, body not responding to reason.

Tom stepped in between us and the fog was replaced by rage. Arabella started to argue and tried to push around him. Eve leaned down to check on me but whatever she saw had her herding everyone out of the room and away from the monster on her kitchen floor.

"Arabella, honey, we need to leave. You too, Acacia. Now." Another cough but Tom was quickly moving her away from me.

He shut the door but I could still hear him. "No, Arabella, you need to listen to me. There are things I haven't told you."

Chapter Eight

Eve circled the airport while I went inside to pick up Rowan. We needed a minute to cover a few things before I let him anywhere near my sister. Don't get me wrong, I liked Rowan, but he's more than a little bit of a flirt.

The airport hadn't changed since I was there two weeks ago. Sheep-people walked around aimlessly and children ran unsupervised. The restaurant's burnt cooking oil permeated the air with an acrid odor. I turned and covered my nose.

"There he is." Rowan wrapped his arm around my shoulders and attempted to kiss my cheek.

"Get off me, you idiot."

Rowan laughed. "Come on, bruv. Is that any way to welcome your best mate? Now, where do I pick up my bag?"

He turned toward baggage claim and started off without me. I quickly followed as Rowan put his arms around and initiated a conversation with two women he'd clearly met on the flight.

"Rowan, a word," I said a bit too loudly.

He blew one woman a kiss and held up his hand like a phone and mouthed *call me* before turning back my way. His hazel eyes ringed in gold twinkled with more mischief than I could currently tolerate. Time to knock him down a peg.

"The correct lingo is text me, not call me. Your age is showing."

"Well, fuck me," Rowan said then winked. "Makes the ladies think I'm retro, instead of old."

His devil may care attitude matched his early twenties look with almost too long sandy brown hair currently tucked under a driving cap. His medium build and average height made him unassuming but his fashion sense was extremely off-putting, at least to me. Considering he was over a hundred, I let it slide most days.

"Speaking of which, Eve is off limits." We had started walking toward baggage claim again. "She may be an adult but just barely, and considering the age gap, that's still pedophilia in my book."

"I'm not responsible for who falls in love with me." Rowan held up his hands when I opened my mouth to set him straight. "Alright, I'll tone it down but only because you're my best mate. Still, I can't promise nothing."

Rowan rushed to the front seat when Eve pulled up to the curb. "Hello, Beautiful."

Eve's cheeks burned red and she stuttered. "H-Hi, R-Rowan. It's nice to meet you."

"Get in. Eve's getting cold," I prompted.

Rowan and Eve hit it off immediately, chatting the whole way back to her condo. I gritted my teeth and tried not to punch his face through the windshield. I'd have to watch him like a hawk.

"We didn't have much time to prepare the guest room," Eve explained, flipping on the bonus room's light.

My guess was correct. Eve had rushed out to buy a futon with a red and green plaid cover. A new lighthouse lamp sat on the small matching dresser. She had even found a framed print of some random field in Wales to put on the wall. Luckily, the guys who installed my window block had left the remaining supplies. The two of us got that up pretty quickly since this was the smallest room with only one window.

“Ah, Eve,” Rowan gushed. “This reminds me of an adorable bed and breakfast back home. Too bad it was destroyed years ago.”

Eve beamed with delight. “Can I get you something to drink? Tea, perhaps?”

Rowan put his arm around her waist and led her up the stairs. “Never was much of a tea man. Got any good stout?”

I said, “She’s not twenty-one” at the same time she said, “We picked some up today. I hope you like them. If you have a brand you prefer, I can get more tomorrow.”

* * *

Eve had a holiday party at the university the following evening so Rowan and I were left to our own devices. He had been laying it on pretty thick with Eve but mostly kept his hands to himself. Worst case, I could always kill him but he wasn’t worth the punishment.

“Where do all the hotties hang out?” Rowan asked about five seconds after Eve left.

“Why in any universe would you think I know the answer to that question?”

He shrugged. "It's beyond stale up here. You must have something to do at night. Unless you've been a naughty boy."

I took a long drink of my wine before answering. The three of us had watched the late-night news before Eve went to bed last night. There was a story about the murder of a local councilman possibly being related to the death of two sex workers earlier this month. Rowan had grinned like a fool when the newscaster switched to an update on the flu.

"I have no idea what you are talking about. You know why I am here."

Rowan lifted his beer then put down the empty bottle with a frown. "To relax and see your sister. Bull shite. You are here because of the one that got away. Have you seen her? How's that going?"

"Is that why you're here? Seraphine thinks I'm out for revenge?"

"Wouldn't you?"

I nodded. It was the easiest explanation. "I don't want to kill her, never did. My mortal life seems like wasted time when I look back on it. Now that time doesn't matter, I've shifted focus."

"From murder to?" Rowan prompted when I didn't elaborate.

"Seraphine is the worst kind of helicopter parent. She gives us this wonderful gift then keeps us from having any fun." I drained the last of my wine. "Let's go find some of these "hotties" you can't seem to live without. This conversation is going nowhere and I haven't eaten anything in days."

Rowan slapped his thighs and stood. "That's more like it."

We walked the few blocks to one of the nicer clubs but Rowan was having none of it. He was looking for a hole in the wall where the once-beautiful went to reminisce about better days. I'd found a few during my evening walks so we headed to the closest one.

The lighting was dim, cigarette smoke clouded the air, and my shoes stuck to the floor. This place had Rowan written all over it. A small stage and dance floor were tucked in the back corner, both currently empty. Only a handful of patrons remained at the late hour. Rowan made friends with the bartender immediately when he handed her his black Amex card with his order. She stepped away to start the tab.

"Make sure this guy never has an empty glass, will ya, Love?" he said, slapping me on the back.

Two shots of tequila were set in front of us. "From the ladies at the end," the bartender explained.

The two women that waved were older than my mother, quite a bit older. I'm sure they had been real knockouts in their day, but that day was long gone. Rowan picked up both shots and headed their way. I took residence on the stool in front of me.

"Not only is your glass empty, but you don't even have one." The bartender stood in front of me with a fist resting on her hip.

"Do you have any cinnamon tequila?" Another memory floated to the surface.

She rummaged around under the bar for a few minutes. "You're in luck. My son got me several bottles of this at the PX a few months back. I've got two left."

She poured me a shot and I enjoyed the slow spicy burn. "How much for both bottles?"

She cocked her head to the side. "It's about forty bucks a bottle but I get nearly sixteen shots outta that so you're looking at two-fifty for the pair. And that's cheap considering I'm not sure I can get more."

I smiled at her then at Rowan. He was sitting between the older women singing an old sea shanty. Even the old man sitting a few tables away was nodding along to the tune. That Brit was the Pied Piper of ass.

"Put it on the card and give yourself a nice tip." I picked up the open bottle then said, "Can you wrap the other one up for me? It's a gift."

I joined Rowan and his dates with the open bottle. Tonight was about convincing Rowan nothing was amiss. I'd play his game so he could go back to report to Seraphine sooner rather than later. I felt a little bad that some kid wouldn't be spending this holiday with his grandma but then again, any self-respecting grandma wouldn't try to hook up with men less than half their age.

Chapter Nine

"Did you finish your Christmas shopping?" I asked Eve over dinner.

She looked at the tree then chewed before answering. "Too late now."

I smiled at her. She'd spent all day wrapping while I slept and now brightly colored packages under the tree spilled out into the room. It didn't help three large boxes had arrived from our parents this afternoon.

She checked her phone again. Apparently, Acacia's parents held a big Christmas Eve party with family and friends every year. This would have been Eve's second year with them but she insisted on staying home with me. Tom had called yesterday to apologize about Arabella's outburst and promised they would both be at Christmas dinner. How much had he needed to persuade her to agree to that? He was doing half the work for me.

"You should have gone to the party, Eve. I don't want you to miss out because of me."

Instead of answering, she took another bite. Her dinner last night had consisted of everything left in her fridge to make room for her Christmas party treats. The thing was now packed with ham, turkey, a smattering of winter vegetables, fresh cranberries, drinks, and of course a larger version of that delectable cheesecake. Tonight, she was enjoying a frozen pizza since everywhere but gas stations were closed for the holiday.

"It's fine. I need to get to bed if I'm to start cooking on time. Who knew rolls took that many hours to make!"

"I am more than willing to help and can get the rolls rising before you even wake up. It's not like my Christmas Eve is fully booked."

Eve gave me a sad smile and conceded. "You can help with the rolls, but that's it. I need someone to play DJ and make sure everyone has a drink."

"I know. I know. You've told me a hundred times." I chuckled.

"You did tell Rowan he could have stayed through Christmas, right?"

Rowan had left yesterday, convinced I really was just as boring as I promised to be. He'd be back in two weeks to make sure I stayed that way. Eve may have developed a little crush on my friend and that was not something I was comfortable with.

"He'll be back for New Year's." I internally groaned at the thought.

Eve's phone rang. "Hey, what's up?"

I could hear Acacia's voice on the other line. "The movie's over and people are starting to leave. Arabella is worried about Tom's cough. It's not getting better. She told me to tell you to set up a humidifier. I told her that Victor was full of enough hot air that it wasn't necessary."

Eve grimaced and went into the living room. "That's not very nice, Acacia. I'll see what I can do about a humidifier. How was the party?"

I cleaned up the kitchen while Eve chatted with her friend. I needed a good plan and had less than twenty-four hours to come up with one. My gift to Arabella was perfect until I really thought about it. The present poked holes in my amnesia story but time had run out to come up with anything else.

The cinnamon whiskey and gourmet hot chocolate was wrapped in a red satin bag behind the tree. The necklace I'd fashioned out of her engagement ring sat in my pocket. There it would stay until the right moment.

The only other gift I'd purchased was for Eve. My having to babysit Rowan had made it too late to order anything online and most of the stores closed by the time I was waking up, making shopping at anywhere other than Supermart next to impossible. No one would be getting a gift from me purchased from a Supermart. Ever.

"Victor?" Eve called from the living room.

I found her sitting on the floor next to the tree. "I know we usually wait until midnight but like I said, I need to crash early."

"Of course. Let me grab your gift."

When I came back upstairs with the large box, her face broke into a huge grin. Eve loved Christmas and I loved making her happy. Tomorrow's problems could wait.

"Now I feel bad about your little gift." Eve gently shook the box in her hands.

I placed the large box next to her and kissed the top of her head. "The best gifts come in small packages. You first."

Eve carefully unwrapped her gift but it took her a moment to realize what it was. The Bluetooth sound system could be set up so every room in her house had music. When she figured it out, she jumped up and hugged me.

"Part of the gift is me installing this for you," I said as I returned her hug.

"Thank you, Victor. You're the best."

"Let's make sure it works before I agree with you."

Eve's phone rang and she frowned. "Hi Arabella. Yeah, Acacia called. How's Tom?"

I couldn't hear the response because an idea hit me so hard, the room swayed. Tom had *that* flu. The one killing vampires. He'd been coughing for over a week and if what Acacia said was true, he was getting worse. From our conversation the other night, I knew he wouldn't choose immortality. He'd be selfish and leave Arabella before taking the steps to have her forever.

"I think I have a humidifier. Don't worry. Tom's never sick for very long. I'm sure he'll be feeling better tomorrow. Merry Christmas Eve. Love you."

This time I did hear the reply, "Love you too, Eve. See you tomorrow night."

* * *

It was a long night and I was happy to have the rolls to keep me home. The desire to check to see how bad Tom's condition had gotten was overwhelming. I forced myself to sit and watch black and white Christmas movies until the sun came up. If anyone asked, I couldn't have told them which ones as my mind was racing.

The sun was lightening the sky when I placed the towel over the rolls for the final rise. I set a timer for three hours and headed to my room. Eve would take it from there.

I picked up the gift from my sister. It was a new bottle of the cologne she and I had created together in a little shop in Italy several years ago. That was probably the last time we'd spent any real time together. I'm surprised she even remembered. The scent took me back to that day and I realized I hadn't found anything I'd really liked since.

I emptied my pockets and turned down the bed. When I moved to close the door, Eve appeared in the hallway.

"Merry Christmas," she said with a yawn.

"Eve, you don't have that much to do. Go back to sleep for a couple hours. My gift to you."

She nodded and moved to leave then hesitated. "That's gorgeous."

My eyes followed her gaze. Arabella's necklace sat on the dresser with my wallet and phone. She picked it up and held it to the light. The pink diamond sparkled and the black pearls almost absorbed the light.

"You can't give it to her," Eve said, laying it gently back on the dresser. "At least not yet."

I wrapped my arms around her. "I know. I shouldn't even have it but it's beautiful, just like her, and she deserves beautiful things."

"So do you, big brother," Eve said, hugging me back. "You won't be alone forever. Your someone is out there, just like mine."

I gave her one more squeeze. "Merry Christmas, Eve. Go back to bed. The coffee maker won't come on for another two hours and your rolls don't need you to watch them rise."

Chapter Ten

The house smelled like Christmas when I woke up. The scent of baked bread, ham, cinnamon, and cloves filled the condo. Not eating tonight was going to be absolute torture. To make sure I wasn't entirely left out of Eve's dinner extravaganza, we had picked up some fancier wine and beers for tonight using my real ID instead of her fake one. She didn't need to get busted over the holidays.

I quickly showered and dressed. Eve had told me dinner would be a casual affair so I stuck with comfort, yet still ended up in all black. The tiny dab of the new cologne made me smile. I could make it through dinner and maybe my brother would be dead by New Year's, making my long-term plans much easier.

"Eve, everything smells amazing," I said as I walked up stairs.

Acacia was once again sitting in the giant bean bag. This time she was folding napkins into fancy coils before adding a napkin ring. Only Eve's version of casual would include napkin rings.

"Merry Christmas, Acacia."

Without looking up, she replied, "She won't let you in the kitchen."

I smiled and headed that way but only made it to the table when Eve yelled, "Nope! Music!"

"You did warn me," I said to Acacia and she snickered.

I was scrolling through playlists on my phone when she spoke again. "How does it work, exactly?"

Her curiosity gave me an in. "I can't share everything but what do you want to know?"

"So, you died. Like, actually dead?"

"Yes, that is part of the process but it doesn't start there. There are only a handful of vampires in the world that can turn one into an immortal. They are called living immortals and are very selective since too many people living forever would raise some eyebrows, not to mention some aren't stable enough to handle it."

"And yet, they let you into their little club." Acacia went back to her napkins.

I ignored her jab. "Overall, it's a pretty simple process. You must be invited by one of those select few, approved, and swear your loyalty."

"That's it?"

"The clan leader also has to provide the living vampire their blood three times before their death. Duration in between donations at the living immortal's discretion. Half of those who swear allegiance never make it that long or are forgotten by the living immortal before the process is complete."

"Still seems pretty sketchy. This clan leader, are they like your boss or queen?"

"A little of both actually. As far as I know, they are all very old and even more picky as time goes on."

She opened her mouth to ask another question as Eve emerged from the kitchen. Her face was flushed and her hair was pulled up in a messy bun now leaning precariously to the left. Flour, seasonings, and sauces were flicked all over her apron.

"Victor, you're in charge of stirring the gravy. Acacia, you're finishing the table, including the candles, go with the white ones. I'm going to shower but will be back in fifteen minutes tops." When neither of us moved, she clapped her hands. "Chop, chop!"

An hour later, everything was ready, including Eve. Music was playing at a level which could be enjoyed along with conversation. Acacia had cleaned the kitchen and set the table. I had kept the food moving. It was almost enjoyable.

There was a knock on the door and I took a deep breath. *Here goes nothing.* I had to convince everyone, including Arabella, that I was fine, that everything was fine. I tipped back my full glass of wine and drained it before Eve even made it to the bottom of the stairs.

"Smooth," Acacia said from behind me.

"Merry Christmas!" Eve welcomed Tom and Arabella.

I could hear the rustle of paper, coats, and boots getting removed. Eve bounded up the stairs with an armload of gifts. Her white fuzzy sweater dress almost glowed in all the twinkling lights.

Arabella ascended the stairs slowly and took several seconds to take in the tree and the stockings Eve had made for each of us. Her eyes lingered on the flames dancing in the fireplace, making the gold irises almost glow. Her dark green sweater and black jeans hugged her curves in all the right places.

"Merry Christmas, Arabella." I'd been standing near the fireplace but somehow, she hadn't seen me.

She startled a bit when I spoke then studied me with narrowed eyes. No doubt Tom had brought her up to speed on my rebirth and the changes that went along with it. I wanted so much to touch her but I stayed still, pulling back my persuasion. Now wasn't the time.

"Merry Christmas, bro."

Tom finally joined us in the living room and came in for a hug. Arabella flinched again when we touched. I noticed Tom felt warm, warmer than usual. Eve bounced in then and wedged herself between us, arms around our waists.

"Who's hungry?" she asked.

"Starving," I replied, not breaking eye contact with Arabella.

She looked away. "I-I need to use the bathroom first."

The sound of the button lock was a familiar sound, followed by running water. She cursed under her breath then the water abruptly shut off. Another curse. It appeared Arabella was just as nervous about tonight as I was.

Acacia knocked on the bathroom door. "Are you okay in there?"

Arabella came out holding the faucet handle. "Don't worry, I know a good plumber."

The sisters shared a laugh then headed to the table. Eve had gone all out, but she'd never been known for subtlety. Her table looked like a picture in a magazine. Everything was in the same white, silver, and crystal theme. The dishes were white China with tiny silver snowflakes around the rim. There were two bottles on the table: red wine and sparkling cranberry juice for our underage participants. Tom's favorite beer sat near the end of the table.

I frowned when I noticed there was no table setting for me, just a wine glass. I snuck a look at Acacia who was suddenly too busy to make eye contact. *Teenagers!* Instead of saying anything, I helped Eve bring out the last-minute items.

Conversation consisted of Eve and Acacia's griping about school and Tom talking about his upcoming tour. Arabella was uncharacteristically quiet, only contributing when necessary but kept glancing at my empty place setting. No one else seemed bothered, even with my earlier statement of being famished.

As the girls cleared the table and filled the dishwasher, Arabella took Tom downstairs where there was less chance of eavesdropping. Luckily, I could still hear everything from the living room.

"What's with Victor?"

"He probably feels bad about freaking you out when we arrived," Tom said.

"No, I mean, why didn't he eat anything?"

"Oh, that," he said, then paused. "Victor's on a liquid diet."

Arabella was quiet for a few seconds and I could almost see her chewing her lip in thought. My brother was the king of holding back uncomfortable truths. She knew exactly what I meant when I said I was famished. What she may not know is that I'd kill just about everyone here for one more taste. I finished my glass of wine and pulled up the holiday playlist. "Frosty the Snowman" was a bit too cheerful at the moment.

"Let's go enjoy the rest of the party. Eve made mulled cider and is dying to open her gifts," Tom said, leading Arabella back upstairs.

Eve announced it was time for presents so the focus turned back to her, and for once I was grateful. The tension was getting a bit thick, even for my liking. I had suggested she open her gifts from our parents early so everyone didn't have to wait but she had insisted on spending her time cooking.

Everyone was thrilled with their gifts. I felt a little guiltier about not having any for anyone but again, I seemed to be the only one who noticed.

"Acacia did the stockings," Eve announced as Acacia got up to hand everyone theirs.

I peeked in and the first thing I saw was a big bottle of sunscreen. I quietly put the entire thing behind my chair. When I caught her eye later, she didn't even try to hide her laughter. My gift to her apparently had been my continual embarrassment for the evening.

Eve returned from the bathroom a few minutes later. "What happened to my faucet?"

Arabella grimaced. "That was me, sorry. I'll buy you a new one and replace it tomorrow."

Eve laughed and gave her a hug. "Thank you. I hated that ugly thing. We can go together and get one that isn't hideous."

Everyone was preoccupied with their presents. Eve wanted to download her new music right away. Acacia followed her downstairs for some printer paper so she could test her new ink set. Tom excused himself to the bathroom. Arabella and I were suddenly alone.

I reached behind the tree and pulled out the gift I had for her. "It might be inappropriate but I got you a Christmas gift," I said, not offering it to her just yet.

"You're right, it's not appropriate." She seemed to have trouble breathing and was unable to look away from me.

I dropped my gaze and realized I had been pouring my emotions onto her. "Sorry. Still getting the hang of this. Your mind must be pretty open."

"You've mentioned that before," she mumbled.

"I have?" I shook my head. "This memory loss thing is really frustrating. If anything, I'd like to remember why our bonding ceremony was interrupted. I must have really loved you…" My voice trailed off when the bathroom door opened.

Tom's coughing interrupted my confession. Now that I listened closer, his breathing sounded labored too. When he appeared in the living room, his skin was paler than usual and his cheeks were red while his lips were almost colorless.

"I hate to be a party pooper but I don't feel very well." He started coughing again.

Eve thundered up the stairs at the sound and handed him a bag of lemon cough drops. "Go home and rest. You have an important date in two weeks and you need to be in tiptop shape."

"I'll take good care of him," Arabella promised and slipped her arm around his waist. He shivered slightly.

"Merry Christmas, Eve. Thanks for the party. I'll give you a call about that faucet," Arabella said, leading Tom to the top of the stairs.

"Don't worry about it. Just make sure he's better for the wedding," Eve instructed.

I hadn't moved from my chair by the fireplace but had re-hidden the gift behind the tree. Arabella looked like she wanted to say more but Tom's coughing caught her attention again.

"Merry Christmas, Victor," she said finally.

"Until next time." I replied, standing in a single fluid motion. "Arabella."

She swayed a bit but I couldn't tell if it was my persuasion or because of Tom's weight. At this point, she was almost carrying him. He stopped at the top of the stairs and had another coughing fit. When he pulled his hand from his mouth, it was red with blood.

"Oh my God!" Eve exclaimed.

I rushed over and really looked at him. He smelled of death already. I pushed myself under his other arm and quickly carried him down the stairs and out the door toward Eve's car. I heard Arabella scrambling to put on her shoes and coat.

As I set Tom in the passenger seat, she covered him with his coat.

“I’m taking him to the ER. Get in or meet us there.”

She pursed her lips as tears rimmed her eyes. I didn’t need to use any persuasion. She was as scared as I was. Suddenly losing my brother wasn’t part of the plan. I didn’t have to lose everything to win this time. There had to be a way to keep them both.

I just needed to find it.

Chapter Eleven

The hospital was about a mile away but the short trip felt like an eternity. I'd seen it when I'd first arrived in town. Tom's wet gasping was punctuated by more coughing. He shivered against the cold of the car as I pulled into the 'Ambulance Only' area. Arabella was out of the car before I'd even stopped. She wrenched open the passenger door and gently pulled Tom out as hospital security stepped from the building. One look at Tom and they backpedaled for a wheelchair.

Arabella looked at me and I nodded at her silent thanks. She basically carried Tom to the wheelchair and lashed out at the help as if they were slowing her down. I would have smiled if I wasn't so worried. The steering wheel creaked under my grip.

After a forced deep breath, I guided the SUV to the ER parking. A plan was forming in my mind. It could save Tom, but I would risk losing Arabella forever. I wasn't ready to live in a world without my twin and I wasn't sure I'd ever be ready to live in a world with her. This wasn't how it was supposed to happen. Time was paramount.

The phone in my pocket buzzed, pulling me from my thoughts. Looking at the screen, I focused on the text from Eve.

Arabella took her keys and you have my car. It's too cold to walk so I'm waiting for an Uber. Keep me posted.

I shot a quick reply. *Arabella took Tom inside. I'm parking. Don't hurry. I'll let you know when we know something.*

I opened my contacts and pressed Seraphine's people. The line rang until it went to voicemail. Once, twice, three times. *Fuck!* I punched the steering wheel, feeling it tilt off center. I scrolled through my contacts again and pressed call.

As soon as the line connected, I started speaking. "Set up an audience with Seraphine for tomorrow night for you, me, and a guest. I don't care what strings you have to pull or favors you have to cash in. Fucking, do it."

"Happy Christmas, to you too, Arsehole," Rowan replied.

"I'm serious. This is life or death." I paused. "Rowan, please."

The other line was quiet so long, I thought he'd hung up. Pulling the phone away from my ear, I could see the call was still going.

"Anything for my best mate. Can you tell me what's going on?"

"Yes, but not now. I'll see you soon. Oh, and I'm going to need the jet and one of the guest houses."

I stuffed my phone back in my pocket and focused on the inside of the windshield. The passenger side was covered in tiny flecks of blood. Without hesitation, I stepped out into the cold, stealing myself for the crowded emergency room. The smell of bleach and death greeted me when the automatic doors rolled open.

A woman comforted her crying son as he held up his burned arm. A frat boy with no eyebrows scowled at his phone. An elderly man napped in the corner. Several vampires, separated from the rest, coughed painfully, reminding me why I was here.

"Excuse me, Miss."

The registration desk nurse held up her finger and continued speaking into the phone. After a couple minutes, she hung up and pointed to the sign in sheet.

"Sign in and we'll call you when it's your turn."

"I'm not here for me. My brother just came in through the ambulance bay."

Another nurse stepped up behind her. "You look just like him. He's being admitted but he's only allowed one visitor and his wife is already with him."

My jaw clenched when she said wife and I desperately wanted to correct her. That was a battle I hadn't lost yet. Instead, I let out my breath and let persuasion seep into my words.

"I'm sure she's about ready for a break. Why don't you take me back to his room?"

The second nurse's eyes glazed slightly but she nodded then pressed the button to unlock the door. The first nurse frowned slightly but quickly turned back to her ringing phone.

I pushed the door open before anyone else questioned why I was going back so quickly. The nurse walked past several beds with curtains drawn. Coughing or crying was heard by each. I was beginning to worry when we exited the curtained rooms into the main hospital.

"He's in room 235." She pointed then hesitated with a confused look on her face.

"Thank you." I noticed her badge. "Marie, you can't know how worried I am about my dear brother."

The glazed look returned and she smiled. Tom's coughing pulled me from her and toward room 235.

"Arabella, you need to leave. You don't want to see this," a voice spoke.

"I'm not leaving! Stan, please." The agony in her voice made my steps slow.

I stepped into the doorway. Arabella stood against the wall, arms folded around herself. The curtain was pulled so I couldn't see Tom, just silhouettes of the hospital staff moving around. Ripping plastic sounded followed by gagging.

Arabella turned her head toward the door and closed her eyes. When she opened them and focused on me, my heart would have stuttered if it could. The pain in her expression was something I understood. In that moment, I would have given anything to ease her suffering. She was losing the love of her life and was helpless to stop it.

My feet seemed rooted in place until she closed her eyes again and tears slid down both cheeks. I stepped close and pulled her to my chest. I expected her to push away but instead she grasped me like a lifeline as silent tears shook her body.

"I'm sorry but we only allow one visitor at a time in the ICU."

I turned to the doctor and instantly recognized him from the restaurant with Cassie. He looked from Tom to me and back then furrowed his brow and nodded. They had put Tom on a ventilator, his eyes were closed, and he was hooked up to an IV and several other machines. I noticed his oxygen level and blood pressure were dangerously low.

Arabella's grip tightened my shirt. "I don't know what to do. I can't…"

Her words broke my heart all over again. She was pleading to a man she hated because she, the person who saved everyone, didn't know how to save Tom. I breathed in her scent and for the first time in my life, put someone else's needs before mine.

"Help me save him," I whispered.

She jerked away and sniffed. Her red rimmed eyes narrowed and she seemed to remember to whom she was speaking. She stepped back and cleared her throat as the doctor approached us.

"I'm guessing Tom didn't take my advice about that flu shot." Arabella shook her head. "And I'm also guessing he's part of the high-risk group?"

Arabella nodded again and swallowed hard.

"Doctor," I glanced at his badge, "Doctor Blackwood, what can you tell us?"

"I'm not going to sugar coat this, it's not good. His fever and oxygen level are concerning." He hesitated and his eyes flicked from mine to Arabella's and back. "The next forty-eight hours are critical, but he's here now and his care will be exceptional. We're going to do everything we can."

I glanced at Arabella and her expression was stone. Her earlier breakdown had been reined in. That or she had completely shut down. The rhythmic beeping filled the silence.

I turned back to Arabella. "Stay with him. I'll update Eve and be back soon."

She nodded robotically and pulled a chair to his bedside. When she took his hand, another tear slid down her cheek. She didn't wipe it away. Nurses fussed over Tom and his machines.

Doctor Blackwood motioned his head toward the hallway. I followed him and he carefully closed the door behind us. We walked down the hall until we stood next to an empty nurses' station.

"He doesn't have forty-eight hours, does he?" I asked.

Dr. Blackwood suddenly looked tired. "I can't guarantee he does. His condition is advanced. If he'd come in earlier, maybe."

My eyes darted back to Tom's room. "Do whatever you can."

He regarded me for a few moments. "Arabella is likely to have been exposed but she isn't showing any symptoms. What about you? Have you spent any time with your brother in the last few days?"

My laugh was harsh. "I don't get sick anymore."

He opened his mouth. "I'm sorry. Uh, I don't know your name, but if your twin is this susceptible to this virus, there is a good chance you are too. I'll do what I can to help your brother, but if you start to exhibit any symptoms, you need to come in immediately."

I was not about to explain my condition to this doctor. "Don't worry about me. Just give me those forty-eight hours."

My phone buzzed in my pocket. I used the distraction to end the conversation and turned away from Dr. Blackwood.

I'm here but no one will tell me anything. Where are you?

Give me a minute, Eve. I'll meet you in the lobby. You'll need to stay with Tom.

I put the phone back in my pocket despite the constant buzzing. Eve wouldn't like my plan either but it was all I had. Arabella's plea set my resolve. Now the question was how was I going to convince her to leave Tom's side?

Chapter Twelve

Arabella was speaking softly to Tom when I returned to the room. The nurses had disappeared and the light was low. She gripped his hand and didn't look away from his face when I stopped at the end of the bed.

"Eve's here. She wants to see Tom." She didn't acknowledge my statement. "Arabella, come with me..."

"I'm not leaving." Her voice was flat.

This was going to be the hardest part. Tom was dying and she wanted every second. She adjusted herself so she took his hand in both of hers. Her engagement ring, hanging loosely on her finger, glinted in the dim light.

I quietly left the room and headed down to the lobby. She wouldn't listen to me but if I could convince Eve, maybe she could pull Arabella away long enough for me to explain the plan.

"Victor!" Eve called as soon as I stepped from the elevator.

She all but ran to me. Acacia was nowhere to be seen. "Is Tom okay?"

"Eve, he's as okay as he can be. Let's take a few minutes and get a coffee for Arabella. I need to talk to you."

We followed the signs to the cafeteria. The smell was less than pleasing but I recognized the logo at the coffee cart so I knew the coffee would at least be tolerable. Cheap holiday decorations hung from the ceiling and walls, but their cheer couldn't penetrate the somber atmosphere.

"Tall white chocolate cinnamon latte and tall caramel mocha," Eve ordered then hesitated. "Did you want something?"

I shook my head but pulled out my wallet to pay for the coffees. Neither of us said anything while we waited for the order to be filled. Eve picked up the white chocolate cinnamon as if to warm her hands then motioned for me to grab the other.

The chairs were hard plastic and the cafeteria was mostly empty. We took a seat by the window. Snow fell slowly in the courtyard. It would have been beautiful in any other circumstance.

"I need to take Arabella to California with me. Tonight."

Eve opened her mouth to protest then stopped as tears filled her eyes. She was smarter than I realized. She knew what I was going to do and she knew why.

"You heard him. He doesn't want immortality." Eve's voice was just above a whisper.

"That was before he was dying, before he had someone to lose."

Her eyes went wide. "You're going to turn Arabella too. Oh Victor, don't do this. There has to be another way."

I hated what I did next but I needed her to convince Arabella to go with me. Persuasion seeped into my voice. "Eve, this is the only way to save Tom. I need you to stay with him. Arabella is the only one who can convince him to go through with this. If she's already on her path to immortality and he truly loves her, he'll join her."

Eve's eyes glistened with tears and she rolled her coffee cup between her hands. "I don't want to lose him either."

"Then help me. Arabella won't leave him and she doesn't trust me. You need to make her understand this is the only way."

Half an hour later, I stood guard at Tom's door while Eve spoke with Arabella. I'd been texting back and forth with Rowan arranging for the jet to pick us up just after two in the morning. My watch told me we were running out of time. If we didn't leave soon, I wouldn't be able to get off the plane until the sun went down again. Both Tom and I were now racing the clock.

Eve's voice rose in volume. "Arabella, when have I ever asked you for anything? You were meant to be my sister and that will never happen if, if… I can't lose my brother. Please."

Eve's sobs tore at my heart because I knew she spoke the truth. My sister never asked anyone for anything. She was always the one giving. She was the one who would risk it all for the ones she loved. Well, maybe not the only one anymore.

The door opened and I stepped aside. Arabella raised her chin, rolled her shoulders back, and looked at me. Really looked. It was clear her emotions were at war. Hatred, mistrust, despair, then hope. When Eve's sobs reached us again, she finally broke eye contact to close her eyes and I knew I'd won.

I opened my mouth to speak but she held up her hand. "Give Eve her keys. I need to walk back to her place to get my car and to clear my head. I haven't decided anything yet and I won't let you make decisions for me ever again."

She'd walked halfway down the hall before she turned back. "Do you need an invitation or something? Get a move on."

I rushed into Tom's room, glancing at his sleeping form for half a second before pressing Eve's keys into her hand and kissing the top of her head.

"Text me with any changes. Don't call unless…"

She bit her lip and nodded before laying her head on Tom's bed. I knew she wouldn't leave his side. *Some Christmas*, I thought as I hurried to follow Arabella to the elevator.

* * *

Arabella's driving was even more terrifying on the frozen roads but at least I'd walk away if we crashed and I think she was too angry to die at the moment. I'd grabbed a few things at Eve's when we'd picked up the car then swung by her house. She didn't let me in but I suggested she pack an overnight bag. She came out with a duffle telling me she was going along with my plan without actually putting it into words.

I checked my phone. We had ten minutes. Luckily, we didn't have to go through security or wait for other mindless travelers to board the plane. The jet was waiting for the two of us. A thought flickered through my mind of taking her somewhere tropical where it could be just us but reality made me shake my head. She'd hate me forever if I let Tom die.

"Keep heading left," I instructed as we approached the airport.

She sighed heavily and continued past the main terminal to a gated area. A man in a yellow safety vest pushed the gate open to let us pass. Arabella pulled to a stop next to a line of other vehicles.

"You're serious? A private jet? Of course. What else could make this any more bizarre?" Arabella gripped the steering wheel, and I wondered if she was backing out.

"We're kind of in a hurry," I reminded her as I opened the door.

Her expression faltered and the pain surfaced for a second before she blocked it again. She didn't want to leave but she understood the need for haste.

"As long as I don't have to sit by you." She grabbed her bag from the back seat and roughly opened her door.

The jet's cabin had four sets of four seats arranged facing each other. The tan leather was soft and still held a smell of newness. Rowan had really come through. Well, maybe I should wait until he confirmed our meeting with Seraphine before I praised him too much. I checked my phone again but still no message.

Arabella sat in the set of chairs on the opposite side, facing away from me. She too had her phone in her hand and was texting furiously. My guess was she was getting an update from Eve.

"The flight isn't long. We should discuss the plan," I offered.

She kept her back turned and rested her head against the window. I couldn't push her and wouldn't use my persuasion. She had to do this on her own or she would never trust me. Instead, I put my head back and closed my eyes.

The next thing I knew the captain was telling us we were landing soon. When I opened my eyes, Arabella was curled up in her seat asleep. Carefully, I moved so I was sitting across from her. Her lashes were darkened by the makeup she'd worn to Eve's party, cheeks slightly pink since she'd not removed her coat. My God, she was the most beautiful thing I'd ever seen.

The plane bumped slightly during landing. She opened her eyes but didn't sit up right away, just stared ahead blankly. The hardened shell reforming as well as her resolve. Her expression said everything.

"I said I didn't want to sit by you," she finally spoke as she sat up and stretched.

I chuckled then handed her a bottle of water. "Don't worry, I've only been here a few minutes. Grab your bag. It's time to go."

Chapter Thirteen

Rowan had a car waiting for us and I was disappointed when Arabella didn't even bat an eye as she crawled into the two-seat Beamer. She just stared out the window as I drove toward the guest house. It was one of many Seraphine had throughout the valley. This one was the least intimidating, while still meeting my daytime needs. I frowned when I realized it catered to my kind, not Arabella's. We were making good time, so I pulled into a 24-hour market and put the car in park.

"Why are we stopping?" Arabella squinted through the rain.

"We need to get some food for you."

She slouched back into her seat. "I'm not hungry."

Not to be deterred, I opened my door. "Maybe not now but you will be by tomorrow and there isn't anything at the house."

She crossed her arms and stared out the passenger window. Repressing a sigh, I headed into the store alone. She was worried about Tom but I was worried about her. She needed her strength when she met with Seraphine. Hell, I needed strength for what I was about to ask. The list of protocols I was breaking kept growing by the minute.

Picking up a basket, I headed to the wine aisle. I picked two bottles then headed to the small produce section. A container of mixed melon, orange juice, bagels, and cream cheese joined the wine. I stood in the freezer section debating my next move but again, I put her ahead of myself. Pulling open the glass door, I retrieved a carton of ice cream.

Arabella hadn't moved when I returned to the car. The sky was starting to change colors. I needed to hurry to the house and talk while I was still able. The rain clouds wouldn't be any protection once the sun peeked over the horizon. There was so much I needed to tell her.

I took the exit that led to the guest house and Arabella drew in a shaky breath. It took me a second to realize why; she thought I had been taking her to my home. I held my tongue and kept driving. She visibly relaxed when I pulled up to the small ranch style house and pressed the button to open the garage door.

We sat for a moment in the dim light before she spoke. "Thank you."

"You need to eat."

She shook her head. "Thank you for that too, but that's not what I meant."

"Don't thank me yet. This isn't going to be easy. Let's get inside and talk. If at any time you change your mind, just say the word and I'll take you back." I hesitated for a moment then added, "I'll promise to take you back *after* sunset but that's one of the things we need to talk about."

The house looked simple but was built for my kind. The windows had light block shielding that automatically rose just before sunrise and lowered after sunset. Seraphine would know I was here. All the guest houses were wired with cameras and motion sensors, not that anyone would ever be able to find them.

I placed the grocery bags on the counter and Arabella started putting the items away automatically. "Caramel swirl, huh? I thought you didn't remember anything."

I couldn't help but smile. "Some things are coming back. I'm going to have some wine. Do you want any?"

She lifted the ice cream and shook it, indicating her choice. I opened a drawer and handed her a spoon. After pouring a glass of wine for myself, I headed into the living room.

Arabella sat on the couch, tucking one foot under her as she sat. The familiarity of it made me hesitate. While it was true that I didn't remember everything, I did remember the little things. I shook my head. This was not the time to reminisce.

Arabella took a big bite of ice cream before speaking. "This is your shit show."

"I need to know what Tom told you about my rebirth. We don't have a lot of time so I don't want to repeat myself."

"Let's see." She took another bite and tapped her spoon in the air with each detail. "Acacia stabbed you. You died. Now you're on a liquid diet, sleep all day, and somehow seem to have convinced everyone that you are more human now that you are undead."

I frowned at her choice of words. "So not much, but that's what my brother does. Let's go over the basics. I was turned by a living immortal named Seraphine. To become reborn, not undead.

Please don't use that term when we meet with her tomorrow. It's very rude. To become reborn, there are steps, some of which we are going to have to rush to save Tom, and you."

She sat forward and lowered her spoon. "What about me? This isn't about me."

"Tom isn't going to go through with this unless you do too." She opened her mouth to protest but I pushed on. "This life is not for everyone. True, you gain things but you also lose them. I'm stronger than before and heal quickly, for the most part. I won't age and my body won't change no matter how much I drink or workout. You mentioned my sleeping all day. I do this because I can't be in the sun and can't recover from prolonged sunlight. It's one of the few things that can actually kill me permanently. I can't eat food without having to force myself to throw it up later. And I need human blood to stay healthy. Healthy isn't the right word but you understand my meaning."

She put the lid back on the container and set it aside. "There goes my appetite. What else? How does the rebirth process actually work?"

"Normally, you are approached by a living immortal, or by their people, and invited in. This is the first line I'm crossing by bringing you to Seraphine. Once you are accepted by the immortal, they have to share their blood with you three times." I paused to take a long drink, not wanting to tell her the last part. "And you have to swear fealty to them for the rest of your immortal life."

"Nope. Not gonna to happen. Take me back." I grimaced and she put her hand to her forehead. "That's not the worst thing. There's more?"

"Seraphine has never invited or accepted a first-generation vampire. You and Tom will have to be a package deal. She's going to want him because he's like me. She can use him. She won't see why you're so important."

"Sounds like your mother. Once again, my lack of genetics are fucking up my life. Or in this case, my death. Wait, do I have to die?"

I reached out toward her but she sat back. "No. You will die someday and that will complete the process but you can choose when it happens. Or, in my case, a bit sooner than planned."

Arabella chewed her lip for a few minutes, thinking about my words. Several times, she looked like she was going to ask more but stopped herself. I could feel the sun coming up like a weight pressing down on me. The last thing I needed to tell her may end this whole endeavor.

"There's a reason Seraphine doesn't select first generations. Most can't handle the transition, but we can test it."

"What kind of test?" When I didn't answer right away, she asked again. "Victor, what kind of test?"

This was it. The deal breaker. I pulled back every bit of my persuasion before I spoke. This had to be one hundred percent her decision. She had to know the risk. She had to choose to trust me.

"You'll have to take my blood to see if your body rejects it." She started to shake her head and stand but I wasn't backing down, anger making my words harsh. "Do you think this isn't torture for me? I'm choosing to save my brother and lose my soul mate. I am bound to you and not being with you is killing me. Controlling my deepest desires while you take my blood and feel nothing in return is worse than death. But I would do it. I *will* fucking do it because this isn't about me!"

She stood looking down at me, fists and jaw clenched. "I never wanted anything from you, Victor."

"I know." I looked down at the carpet. "I'm truly sorry."

Her footsteps retreated into the kitchen and I heard the freezer open and shut. I listened as she picked up her duffle bag and headed further into the house. She found one of the bedrooms and shut the door, pushing the button lock behind her. Some things never changed.

* * *

The sun was still up but something roused me from my sleep. The room was nearly pitch black except for the digital clock on the nightstand, which read 3:18. I lay still and listened to figure out what woke me up. The bed dipped on the other side and I rolled in that direction.

"Why are you really doing this?" Arabella whispered. "Don't lie."

She was sitting on the bed next to me and I longed to pull her close, to have her lips on mine. I suddenly needed her body against me to keep from falling apart. I'd tried to convince myself this was about saving Tom and putting Arabella's needs before mine but that was a lie. My eyes burned and if I could still cry, I know a tear would have escaped. When I finally spoke, it was the most honest truth I've ever uttered.

"I can't live in a world without you, even if you aren't mine."

She was motionless and silent for what felt like an eternity. "What happens if I don't do this test?"

I sighed. "If Seraphine offers her blood, you could die right then and there. I haven't been immortal very long and I'm not, nor will I ever be, a living immortal. Her blood is so much more potent than mine."

I heard her swallow and shift closer. "Just a test. If you try anything funny, I will toss your ass outside into the sun."

"I would expect nothing less."

While she could see fairly well in the dark, I could see her as if it was midday. She was wearing what looked like an old concert t-shirt and thin cotton shorts. The darkness couldn't disguise her fear or the war she was currently battling within herself. She wasn't afraid that I would do something, she was afraid she would.

I sat up and rubbed a hand through my hair. This was going to be hard on both of us but I wouldn't risk her life. Her hatred toward me was strong; she'd be able to stop and leave. I'm not sure I'd ever recover but it was a chance I had to take.

She gently took my arm across my body in her hands and bit down on my wrist. My brain exploded in euphoria and I knew the rest of my body was responding as well. I lost the ability to speak, to think, or even breathe for a few moments. Instead of fighting my response, I let it crash over me for I knew it would never come again.

I tried to move my arm away but she held tighter, pulling harder on my blood. If she didn't stop now, I knew I wouldn't either. My voice came out raspy and slurred.

"Arabella, I think that's plenty."

When she lifted her head, I was frozen in place. The gold of her irises glowed like fire, blood stained her lips and a single drop slid down her chin. She reached up and licked her fingers clean. I'd never seen hunger like this, not in her or anyone. If I'd thought she was beautiful before, the creature before me was a true Goddess.

"Arabella, are you alright?"

Her voice was too low to catch the first time but she moved to straddle my lap. "More," she whispered against my neck.

I wanted to give her more. I longed to give her everything but I wasn't doing this for me and she wasn't in her right mind. She'd hate me even more-and herself-if I didn't stop this now.

"You've had enough." I put my hands on her hips to lift her back onto the bed.

With a flurry of motion, we were both on the floor. She had pinned my arms above my head with one hand and pressed my head to the side with the other then bit down on my neck. My body relaxed on its own because that's what it wanted. My mind was slow to catch up. Her hips pressed down on my erection and I rose to meet her.

“More,” her whisper was almost a moan as she moved across my body and bit again.

Something was wrong. She should have stopped. This wasn’t blood sharing, it was a test to see if she’d survive the transformation. I tried to untangle myself from her again with little progress. She shouldn’t be this strong.

When she relaxed to move again, I grabbed her face in my hands and pressed my lips against hers. I kissed her with passion I didn’t know I had. She melted and returned the kiss. When I pulled back and opened my eyes, I saw hers were glowing again.

She scooted away and laid her head back against the wall. “What happened?”

It took me a moment to find my voice. “I think you passed the test.”

When she opened her eyes again, the glow was gone. Without another word, she stood and left the room.

Chapter Fourteen

My phone buzzed just after six. I attempted to sit up and was reminded of how unsatisfied I'd been when I'd finally been able to drift off to sleep again. I looked around the room and suddenly wondered if I'd dreamt the entire encounter.

I picked up my cell. There were two messages. One from Eve about two hours ago and one from Rowan just now. I opened Eve's first.

No change. Acacia brought me some clean clothes and Christmas music. I couldn't stand listening to the silence anymore.

I sent a reply: *No change is good. We're okay here. I'll know more soon. Stay strong, baby sis.*

My finger hovered over Rowan's message dreading both the idea that he hadn't gotten the meeting or that he had. What if last night had been a dream? Arabella's response made no sense. The sound of the shower starting up gave me time to figure out how to broach the conversation. I pressed Rowan's text.

Ten at the big house. I made the meeting for three of us. Don't be late.

I typed a quick reply: *We'll be there.*

The big house, as Rowan so delicately put it, was about two hours away, without traffic. It gave me a little more time to prepare Arabella for the meeting. Seraphine was easily offended and Arabella wasn't known to mince words. Like an idiot, I just sat in bed and did nothing until the shower shut off.

I stepped out of my room as she opened the bathroom door wrapped in a towel. Her bra straps were visible so I knew she wasn't naked underneath. One look from her and it was clear, I hadn't dreamt our little encounter.

"What the fuck did you do to me?" She rounded on me and I took a step back at the venom in her voice.

"I didn't do anything. We needed to test..."

She pulled off the towel and pointed just to the left of her belly button. "My scar is *gone*. Where you fucking shot me. It's just gone."

I looked at her perfectly sculpted stomach without understanding what she was saying. I'd been lamenting about her being skinny but I was wrong. She looked like she lived at the gym, every muscle was toned without being bulky. It was as if she was a perfect version of herself.

Apparently, she was tired of my staring so she whipped the towel closed again. "Well?"

I shook my head. "I don't know. I haven't shared blood since my rebirth."

"Stupid, selfish asshole! You didn't even know if your blood would kill me. Did you lie about needing the little test on the off chance you might get laid? What is wrong with you? What is wrong with *me*?" She stomped off in the direction of her bedroom but I followed.

"I'm the one who stopped the whole thing! I'm doing this to protect you." She slammed the door in my face, but I immediately pushed it open to be greeted with a pistol aimed between my eyes.

I pulled in a breath, raised my hands, and stepped back. There were other ways to kill an immortal and a bullet to the head was one of them. I hadn't mentioned that last night but I think she figured it out from my response.

I spoke slowly, hoping to not provoke her further. "I am here to save Tom. I need you to do that. Arabella, I would wait an eternity for you but I will never force you to do anything ever again. You have to believe me."

"Then stop," she begged, shoulders sagging a little. "I can almost see your persuasion in the air. It's so strong I can barely breathe."

She was right. When my emotions swung, so did the levels of my persuasion. It was something I was working on but hadn't mastered like I had in life. Right now, I was pleading in front of the woman I loved, who was mostly naked, and my will was permeating everything.

With a nod, I walked to the bathroom, turned the cold water on full, and stepped in the shower. I needed to be in complete control when we met with Seraphine. It was time I pulled myself together and stuck to the plan. The rest could wait.

* * *

Arabella was in the kitchen when I emerged sometime later. She had half a bagel in her hand as she stared at her phone. I was channeling my inner attorney and was all business.

"We're to be at Seraphine's at ten. It will take at least two hours to get there. We need her to listen, so you need to not speak unless directly spoken to. Once she makes up her mind, that is it. We'll leave no matter her decision."

She looked up from her phone and finished chewing her bite. "And if she says no?"

"Like I said, we'll leave."

"I don't think I'm okay with that. I'm here against every bit of common sense and you're telling me she may say no and we'll just walk out? Who does she think she is?"

I adjusted the cuffs on my sleeves, wishing I had asked Arabella to bring something nicer to wear for this meeting. Her ripped jeans and faded pullover hoodie would not help our case.

"Seraphine is one of the only known living immortals left in the US. She is hundreds of years old and is set in her ways. While she adores innovation and technology, she bases herself in formality and control. She can be reasoned with but once she's set her mind, the conversation is over. I've seen people push too far. It is not pretty."

A blob of cream cheese fell onto Arabella's shirt and my control slipped. "Did you bring anything nicer to wear? This is kind of important." She continued to chew and I glanced at my watch. "There's an outlet mall on the way. Finish your food and let's get moving."

"I'm making another for the road."

Arabella picked up the bread knife and sliced the bagel a bit too hard. The knife caught the palm of her hand and the scent of her blood filled the room. She dropped the knife in the sink with a curse then pressed her hand to her mouth. With the other, she dropped the bagel into the toaster and stepped around me.

My nerves were already on edge and her blood was my drug. I was paralyzed in place and felt if I moved, I would drain her dry. When I heard her bedroom door shut, I went to the sink and stared at the knife. The edge held a line of red.

Without thinking, I picked it up and licked it clean. The euphoria from last night started to resurface and my head began to fog. I gripped the sink to keep myself from moving. Footsteps sounded behind me, pulling me back to reality, and I turned on the water in pretense of washing dishes.

"Is this better?"

I took a few seconds to gather myself before turning because I was still floating in the blood haze. She had changed into a dark red sweater dress, not unlike the one Eve had worn the night before, and black ankle boots.

"Much." I turned away and focused on the dishes. "Pack your things, we'll be heading back to Montana after the meeting."

I couldn't let her go and refused to wait an eternity. We'd save Tom and then I would figure out how to make her mine. I don't know what happened when she took my blood but I would do anything in my power to make sure it happened again.

Chapter Fifteen

We headed north, leaving the city proper but didn't speak on the drive to Seraphine's. The frontage road took us away from the highway and other houses. The big house sat on several acres, all of which was surrounded by a thick iron fence. Arabella's eyes went wide when we approached the gate but she still didn't say anything.

We drove for several more minutes before the house became visible through the trees. I'd been here only once before so the view was still impactful. The big house was actually several dwellings surrounding what could only be called a mansion. While the place was impressive, what made it special was the fact there were three floors beneath the main house that were completely sealed off from light. Seraphine could call all her local reborn and accommodate them for some time if she wished.

"Is that a hearse?" Arabella asked as we parked.

The black monstrosity had been fully restored to its former 1970's glory. It fit two coffins, which permanently resided inside. I'm pretty sure the only reason Seraphine tolerated the eyesore was because it was a Jaguar.

"That would be Rowan's."

"Rowan?" Arabella looked from the car to the house then back to me, her bravery slipping.

"He's my friend and the one who set this up for us." I lifted my hand to rest it on her leg but shifted to remove the keys instead when movement caught my eye. "Speak of the devil."

She turned to follow my gaze as Rowan descended the stairs from the house. He had dressed for the occasion, even if his fashion sense was a bit dated. He looked straight out of *Oliver Twist*, top hat and all.

He opened the passenger door and offered his hand. "My lady."

I hurried around as he helped her from the car. "Rowan, this is…"

"Arabella Simon. Nice to meet you," she interrupted.

"Oh, I know, my dear. We know all about you." He smiled and wrapped her arm around his then turned toward the stairs before glancing back at me with a dark look.

I scanned the grounds and outside of the house before following them. It looked empty but I could feel multiple eyes on me. Rowan was regaling Arabella with details of the house and its history. She nodded politely and kept her mouth shut until we stepped inside.

The entryway was designed to be imposing. Cream and gold marble floor, crystal chandeliers, and an arching staircase dominated the space. Fresh flowers were strategically placed, filling the air with their fragrance. A man stood on either side of the door. I recognized one of them from my previous visit. His flat face and gap-toothed grin were hard to forget.

Arabella turned and saw the men. "Um, I need to use the ladies' room?"

Rowan motioned with his arm. "Right this way."

Once she had stepped into the ladies' parlor that led to the restroom, Rowan turned on me. "Are you bloody insane? Why is she here?"

"It's not what you think. My brother is dying. She's here to help plead his case for rebirth."

"Seraphine isn't going to like this. You know how she feels about first generations and the history between you two. You'll be lucky if she doesn't throw you both in the sunroom."

"It won't come to that."

"It won't come to what?" Arabella asked.

Rowan laughed to dispel the tension. "Tell me, Love, do you know Victor's delightful sister?"

I followed Rowan farther into the house as he and Arabella talked about Eve. Discomfort was starting to poke holes in my perfectly laid out plan. Seraphine would want Tom in a heartbeat. He had the same power of persuasion as I plus access to the public like no one had in decades. The unknown was how my living immortal would react to Arabella.

The memory of last night tugged at my mind and I kept trying to push it away. Something about it screamed for us to run from the house. Rowan had led us down a hallway full of paintings said to be Seraphine's ancestors. No one knew if they were actual blood relatives or famous vampires she'd turned over the centuries. There was one that was clearly a direct relation and I stopped in front of it.

Unlike the others, there was no name plate. The man staring back at me was royalty of some kind with hard, uncaring eyes. Seraphine had his nose and lips. I've been told it was her father but I never saw any reason to tempt fate by asking her directly.

The next painting was an enormous rendering of Seraphine in a field of wildflowers. Mountains pierced the sky behind her like nothing we have in the US. Her cherubic features hadn't changed in the time since this was painted until now. Arabella joined me in front of the painting.

"Seraphine in Spring," she read aloud. "That can't be who..."

The door opened at the end of the hall. "She will see you now."

The three of us turned and suddenly I wanted to be anywhere but here. The risk seemed too great. Rowan was right. Seraphine would never accept Arabella and Tom would never agree without his bride-to-be.

Both Rowan and Arabella were already making their way down the hall before I moved to join them. There was nothing else to do. It was too late. I sent a silent prayer to whatever deity may be listening that I hadn't brough us all to our deaths.

* * *

While the rest of the house was decorated in contemporary luxury, this room was all modern. An enormous projector screen covered one wall; multiple gaming systems were neatly arranged along another. A bar, complete with bartender, gleamed opposite the screen while a black leather seating area dominated the remaining space.

Seraphine was playing a dancing game that mirrored her movements on the screen. The music sounded like K-Pop as she whirled in time for a perfect score. We watched and waited until the song ended.

The living immortal glanced my way but quickly turned and spoke to Arabella. “Let’s play a two-player song next. Stand here.”

“I don’t think I’m very good at this kind of game.” Arabella looked from Seraphine to me and back.

“Don’t be silly. Just follow the stick figure in the corner. Your avatar mimics your movements.” She bounced over and pulled Arabella so she was facing the screen.

Seraphine picked a second avatar, which looked too much like Arabella to be a coincidence, then selected another K-pop song and started dancing with Arabella struggling to follow. Rowan tilted his head toward the bar. Seraphine did things in her own time so we would wait until she was ready.

While it appeared our living immortal was ignoring us, I knew she was listening to everything we said. Rowan gave me a warning look to confirm my suspicions. We made small talk about hockey, cars, and weather while we sipped our drinks. Six songs later, the girls joined us at the bar.

“Two ginger ales, please,” Seraphine asked the bartender as she gently dabbed her forehead with a towel.

Arabella was breathing hard and took a proffered towel herself. I felt bad about the long-sleeved sweater dress now. She looked hot and very uncomfortable. Seraphine was wearing a pair of pastel joggers with a matching hoodie adored with a crystal logo I didn't recognize.

"That was so fun. It's nice to know that I'll have a girlfriend to spend lots of time playing games with soon. Shall we sit?" Seraphine gestured to the couches.

Two plates sat on the glass coffee table. One held crackers, cheese, and a knife, the other vanilla cookies. Seraphine picked the second and offered it to Arabella. She took one but didn't immediately take a bite.

"Seraphine, if I may?" I began but she stuck out her bottom lip. It was hard to remember I was dealing with such a powerful being when she acted like a spoiled brat.

"Oh Victor, you're no fun. Always business with you. I'm getting to know my new friend. We will be friends, right, Arabella?"

To Arabella's credit, she was holding her tongue. She used that moment to pop the cookie in her mouth and nod her head in reply. Seraphine clasped her hands together and beamed with joy.

"Okay, boys, you can tell me why you're here while my friend and I have some yummy snacks."

I cleared my throat, which made Seraphine pause while spreading cheese on a cracker. She didn't look up but the tension in her shoulders told me her patience was waning. Despite her outward appearance, she was not happy.

"I know this isn't normal protocol but my brother… My twin brother, Tom, is very ill. We are here today to request his acceptance for rebirth."

The girl turned her ice blue eyes on me and chewed slowly. "Right to the point, as usual. Why should I accept him? What makes him worthy?"

"We both have the power of persuasion plus I know you've heard of him. He's about to embark on a world tour."

She disregarded me with a wave of her arm. "Why are you here, friend? I know you and my dear Victor have some unpleasant memories."

Arabella licked her lips and snuck a glance my way. "The past is the past. I'm here because I love Tom enough to take the steps to become reborn with him."

Seraphine laughed. "I want a new friend but we have a little problem. I don't take charity cases or tagalongs. Tom sounds interesting but I'll have to meet him before I decide anything. However, there is nothing you bring to my table, other than a moment of entertainment."

Arabella's jaw tightened and I knew she was about to say something she couldn't take back so I cut in quickly. "Tom and Arabella are a package deal. He won't agree to the change without her."

"Well, that complicates things, doesn't it?" She sat back and tested the point of the cheese knife with her fingertip. "Did Victor tell you how this process works?"

I started to speak but her look made the words die in my throat. Arabella answered carefully. “He told me that you have to accept me, I mean us, share your blood three times, and we have to swear fealty to you.”

A nasty smile crossed Seraphine’s face. “That’s what he’s supposed to tell you but did he tell you the rest? About how the transformation changes you? About how I will require your blood as part of the oath?”

Arabella frowned at me then looked back at Seraphine. “No. He didn’t mention that.”

“Well, do you still want this life? All the perks,” she gestured around the room, “and all the disadvantages?”

She snapped her fingers and the projector screen withdrew into the ceiling revealing a window behind. One of the men from the main door had entered without my noticing and pulled the shade covering the window. A burnt skeleton hung limply against the glass.

Seraphine snapped her fingers again and the shades were dropped back into place. “It’s all or nothing. What say you, friend?”

I knew what was about to happen but was too slow to stop it. Seraphine slashed at Arabella with the knife, slicing across both forearms where she’d pulled up her sleeves. Flecks of blood flipped off the end and dotted both Rowan and myself. The scent and surprise made us both gasp.

“What the fuck? Why would you do that?” Arabella shouted and moved to get up.

“Sit down!” Seraphine roared. “You didn’t answer my question. What… Say… You…”

My eyes begged her to accept. This was our only chance. The meeting had actually gone better than I imagined but it was do or die time. Literally and figuratively.

Blood trickled down Arabella’s arms onto her skirt, disappearing into the dark fabric. Her teeth were clenched and I could tell she desperately wanted to slap Seraphine down. Every inch of her was coiled to spring.

Seraphine lifted the knife to her lips and said, “Let’s see if you are even worth saving.”

She licked the knife slowly from end to end then closed her eyes. A moment later, her eyes popped open with a small cough followed by another. The knife clattered to the floor and her hands went to her throat. As if in slow motion, her face began to turn gray starting at her lips and moving up one cheek. The gray turned to ash as the skin fell away. Ear piercing shrieks soon filled the room.

For a heartbeat, no one moved. Rowan grabbed my arm then picked up Arabella in a fireman’s carry and sprinted down the hall. The screaming followed us as we made our way outside. Everyone was rushing toward Seraphine as we were running away. I had no idea what just happened but I didn’t want to be anywhere near here when I figured it out.

Chapter Sixteen

"Get in the car!" Rowan dropped Arabella near the passenger door of his hearse.

She obeyed, still bleeding and in shock from what just happened. I veered toward the BMW to grab our bags then tossed them in his car as I crawled in through the back. I barely had the hatch closed before Rowan took off.

With a good yank, Arabella ripped the sleeves off her dress and used them to bandage her arms. The smell of her blood was making my head swim. I couldn't process what had happened in the house due to its pull.

"What in the bloody hell was that, Victor? Why would you bring a living immortal to Seraphine? She has been systematically taking them out for centuries. Are you really that daft, old man?"

Arabella half turned in her seat so she could see us both. "What is he talking about? What just happened?"

It all made sense. I sat back and put my head in my hands. The call of her blood, her perfection, and most of all the reaction to my immortal blood. I was an idiot but how could I have known?

"Victor, answer me!" Arabella yelled.

"She doesn't know. Fuck me. She doesn't even bloody know." Rowan kept repeating.

"Know what? Someone needs to explain what the hell is going on."

I lifted my head and looked at her. "You died when you were shot, didn't you?"

"No!" she snapped back. "I mean, my heart stopped during surgery but only for a few seconds. Clearly, I'm alive and well. Not exactly well, I'm bleeding all over the car but yeah, not dead. I am not dead."

Her final words sounded like she was convincing herself more than me. Rowan continued to mutter under his breath as he got on the interstate heading north. Arabella chewed her lip in thought and I knew she was running back the last day in her head.

"Victor, give me your mobile." Rowan reached his hand back and I slapped it into his palm. He grabbed his from between the seats and tossed them both out the window. "You too, Ara."

Arabella shook her head so I tried to explain. "They'll be tracking us but they don't have your information. You can keep your phone for now."

"You wanna bet your life on that? Did you not see Mr. Crispy in the sunroom? Do you want to end up like him? I sure as hell don't. The only advantage we have is we can travel during the day since we have someone without a sunlight allergy."

His words seemed to snap Arabella out of her shock. "Rowan, tell me what's happening."

He let out a sigh and passed a car before answering. "Ara, my dear, you are a living immortal, like Seraphine, but clearly just reborn. Your blood is both something special and something terrible. No one is meant to live forever. I see that now. Seraphine went mad living so long. She killed the last living immortal in the western hemisphere over a hundred years ago. She thought she was untouchable, so arrogant that she didn't even recognize you for what you are."

"How would she if I didn't even know?" she asked then lifted her hands to her cheek. "Are you telling me my blood did that to her face?"

"Yes, but it's not permanent with all the immortal blood she has at her disposal. You are her worst enemy and our greatest hope. Seraphine was the only option if we wanted to continue to live. You provide another choice and she isn't going to like that. That is, if we can keep you alive, so to speak."

"Oh no. I'm not creating an army of the undead." She turned to me. "Aren't you guys stuck with her anyway?"

Rowan met my eyes in the rear view before speaking. "We can switch alliances but you aren't going to like how it's done. I'll answer your questions but for now, get some sleep. You'll need to take over driving in a couple hours."

I opened her bag and handed her a hoodie for a pillow. All this was news to me as well. I was clearly no longer running the show. Rowan was several steps ahead and saving all our asses.

After Arabella drifted to sleep, the car stayed silent. Rowan and I were both too busy with our own thoughts to speak. About half an hour before sunrise, Rowan pulled off the road at a rest stop. We both got out and stretched. Arabella was still asleep.

"You really didn't know?" Rowan asked and I shook my head. "Jes-us. You're in love with one of the most unique creatures on this planet and you didn't bloody know."

"Shut up, asshole. Tell me how we switch alliances."

Rowan put his hands in his pockets and rolled back onto his heels. "Well, it starts with a blood orgy, which I guess would just be a threesome since there are only three of us…"

I punched him in the arm. "I'm serious. Can we change allegiances or not?"

"Yeah, we can. I did. Seraphine didn't change me but I helped her kill who did."

Arabella opened her door and stepped outside at that moment. I quickly rearranged my features to hide my shock. She tilted her neck from one side to the other and stretched her arms above her head then bent over to touch her toes. Her eyes glowed faintly in the dark when she stood and faced us.

Rowan looked at her then back at me. "Holy Hell. *That*, my dear Victor, should have been your first clue that this woman is more than she seems."

"What should've been your first clue?" Arabella looked down at herself and peeled the shirt sleeves off her arms. The blood had clotted but the marks looked angry and raw.

"Give her a quick sip to fix up those arms then we need to get settled before sunrise."

Rowan headed to the back of the car and popped the hatch. We'd have to ride in the coffins until the sun went down. While I had never suffered from claustrophobia, I was not looking forward to that.

"A quick sip of what, Victor?" Realization crossed her face and her hand went to her stomach. "My scar is gone. It disappeared after I drank your blood. Oh, fucking hell no. I'll wait until they heal normally. Thanks."

Rowan's head appeared around the car. "Sorry. That's not really an option anymore. The longer you are dead, the less you will heal without immortal blood treatments."

"I still think I'll pass."

"It's a cycle, Ara. Human blood feeds the turned immortals to keep them 'alive', the turned immortals then provide their blood to the living immortal to keep them 'alive'. Without turned immortal blood, your heart will stop and you will start to lose everything that makes you *you.* Your mind will break and you'll become the monster of legend surviving in the shadows on stolen blood. If you don't want his, I have plenty to spare."

"Better the devil you know," Arabella mumbled.

Than the devil you don't. I hadn't tried very hard to get to know Rowan and I wondered why he had taken such a shine to me. He was a good friend but she didn't know him and clearly, I still had a lot to learn about the guy.

"Get a move on. Daylight's a' coming." Rowan turned toward the sky lightening in the east.

"It's okay. Barely even hurts." Arabella tried to sound nonchalant rather than as uncomfortable as she looked.

"Now you know what's coming, you can fight it," I said.

She stepped to me and acted like she was giving me a hug. Her lips brushed my neck and teeth broke my skin. The euphoria peaked as the world fell away but disappeared too soon when she stepped back and looked down, avoiding my gaze.

My breathing was all over the place and my pants were suddenly far too tight. When she finally looked up, her gold eyes shone like the sun. I broke eye contact first and reached for her arms. The angry red gouges were already fading to pink. I nodded and headed to the back of the car.

"I'm not sure the lid will close with that stiffy, mate."

"Shut up and get in the car, Rowan."

* * *

"No officer, I'm afraid I don't know how fast I was going." Arabella's voice sounded muffled through the coffin. The cop's reply was too low but I heard her response, "Yes, you're right. I must be more tired than I thought."

I didn't need to open the lid to know the sun was down. I could feel it. Hopefully, Rowan was still asleep and we would get through this without incident. A sharp thump sounded and I wanted to once again strangle that idiot.

This time I did hear when the cop spoke. "Miss, I'm going to need you to open the trunk."

"Officer, I just have my luggage in the back. I'm really tired. There's a truck stop and hotel at the next exit. I promise I'll stop and get some sleep. Can you help me?"

The pause was long enough that I almost opened the lid but then I heard, "Drowsy driving can kill, Miss. I'll follow you to the next exit to make sure you're safe."

There was a thump on the top of the car and footsteps walking away. After a few minutes, the car started moving again. I could hear Arabella mumbling under her breath then the sound of the turn signal. The car stopped, started again, then stopped and the engine shut off.

A moment later, I both heard and felt a smack on my coffin. "Get up, it's well past dark. I need to pee then it's time for some answers."

The car door opened and slammed then I heard Rowan getting out so I waited. For once, I didn't have any answers and that was not a feeling I enjoyed. Somehow, I didn't think Arabella was going to like them any more than I would.

We were parked along the dark side between the hotel and truck stop. The air smelled of diesel and fried food. Getting out of the coffin was a lot harder than getting in. I was glad Arabella wasn't watching when Rowan chuckled at my struggle.

Rowan did a walk around to check his car. I stretched and waited for Arabella's return. After a few minutes, I started to worry. A quick scan told me her bag was missing. I had only taken two steps toward the truck stop when she rounded the corner wearing her jeans and hoodie, a bag of fast food in her hand.

"You need gas and your radio sucks," Arabella announced, moving toward the passenger side door.

"Any word from Eve?" I asked.

She looked at me for a moment as if deciding whether to answer. "No change. Let's get going."

Chapter Seventeen

Once the car was gassed up, Rowan tossed me the keys. I got back on the interstate and headed north. The radio played bad '80s music while Arabella munched on her chicken fingers, burger, and fries. Once finished, she switched the radio off and turned her body toward Rowan in the back.

"Bring me up to speed. You have about five hours to teach me everything you know about living immortals. I've got a fiancé to save."

"Speaking of speed, how did you convince that cop to let you go so easily?" I interrupted, trying to wrap my head around her calm. Over eight hours of being alone in her own head must have answered a few things but there was still so much unknown, for both of us.

Rowan cleared his throat. "That is not where I had planned on starting but it is as good a place as any. Ara, my dear, you used Victor's gift of persuasion."

"I did what now?"

My fingers tightened on the steering wheel waiting for his response.

"Seraphine collects special vampires for a reason. She chose our mutual friend here for his ability to talk people into things or as he likes to call it 'persuasion'. So far all she's done is asked him nicely to do so on his own. What he may or may not have known is when a living immortal takes blood from one of their bound reborn, they adopt, for a short while, their gifts."

"But Victor swore himself to Seraphine, not me."

"Are you sure about that, Love?"

Rowan's question made my gut twist. I'd sworn fealty to Seraphine almost ten years ago and I'd received my third share of her blood about five years after. A lot had happened since then. The most important being binding myself to Arabella. I never made the connection since I clearly became reborn after the binding ceremony believing I was still sworn to Seraphine. Apparently, she thought so as well.

Arabella shifted in her seat but I didn't risk looking at her when she asked, "Can you switch alliances through a blood ceremony like Victor did with me?"

Her unquestioning acceptance of my binding arrangement grated on my nerves. She had no idea what kind of power she held over me and once again, others were making decisions for me as if I wasn't here.

"Sadly, no. I'm not sure how that one bypassed the system and I can't guarantee it would work for me. Let's go back to the beginning, shall we? I met our dear little Seraphine in 1843."

"You lying little prick! You told me you were a hundred and eight," I interrupted.

"Sorry, mate. That's a little white lie Seraphine held me to since, well, we'll get there. Let's just say that I've been with *her* for that long. Now, where was I? Oh yes, 1843. I was working nights in a publishing house when I came across Seraphine one very late night, a girl of wealth in a not so nice part of town. I offered to help her find her way for a small fee. She politely declined and hurried on. Something about her made me recall the brief encounter often.

"Two years later, I was approached by my employer who invited me to his estate for a holiday dinner. It might shock you to learn that I didn't come from money so I jumped on the chance for a hot meal. I worked hard so I didn't question his hospitality as anything more than a genuine thank you."

"This is a nice history lesson but how is this relevant? I've only got a few hours to figure out what the hell I am and how to use it."

"Does she always complain like this?" Rowan asked me then launched back into his story. "For time's sake, I'll give you the abridged version. My employer was a reborn immortal. His sire, a Lord from a nearby province, was at the party. They offered me immortality with wealth and security if I swore my immortal life to this Lord. As I said, nothing in my life had been easy to this point so I immediately accepted. The process you heard was explained to me and we began the steps that very night. Everything was fine for the first couple years, then they started asking me to do things I wasn't comfortable with."

Rowan took a breath and let it out slowly as if choosing his next words carefully. "How do I put this? Let's just say this century didn't come up with the idea of child trafficking for sexual exploitation. My clan and I relocated to the United States in 1911 after a few too many young girls went missing in

England. The same girl I saw in 1843 crossed my path again shortly after. Being an immortal, I thought she must be one too. We became fast friends, or so I thought. Skipping ahead through some very long years to 1918… If you remember, there was a flu going around then too.

"We shared our woes of living so long and being servants to others. How the living immortals were greedy and gluttonous, and we were no better than slaves. I wasn't supposed to mingle with immortals outside my clan but Seraphine won me over with her sweet charm. We knew we'd get caught eventually and after one too many close calls, she told me her truth. She confessed that she was a living immortal and she could set me free.

"We devised a plan, or I should say, *she* devised a plan. I was to bring her to my sire as I would any girl for his pleasure. Once inside, all she needed was for him to take her blood enough to incapacitate him and I would do the rest. This was against my oath and I was afraid that I would die the instant my sire did but she had an answer for that too. She offered me her blood for so many days leading up to the plan and I swore every time my eternal loyalty to her and only her."

Rowan was silent for a time and Arabella shifted anxiously then asked, "After he took her blood, what did you have to do?"

I caught Rowan's eyes in the rear-view mirror and I've never seen more regret. He may not have wanted the immortal life with his old sire but I knew that Seraphine was just as bad, maybe worse in her own way. He wanted to find someone to truly set him free and he saw that freedom in Arabella.

"Immortals, even living immortals, can't survive long without their head." Arabella gasped but he pressed on. "I knew I'd made a mistake when she made me bag the head and bring it with us. She showed me her trophy room with all the heads of other living immortals she'd killed."

"I'm sorry to make you relive that." Arabella reached back and I assumed she took his hand in comfort. "But, Rowan, I don't understand how I'm dead. I mean, I have a heartbeat, eat food, and can walk in the sun. And I'm sorry to be so impatient but I need to know how to save Tom. If I really am a living immortal, how do I make someone undead, I mean immortal?"

He chuckled at her faux pas then answered. "There's the rub. Living immortals seem to be enemies so I don't know how the knowledge is passed on. They surely aren't going to share the secret with one of their reborn. It seems like it's instinct, something you're born with."

Arabella sat back with a huff. "Great! F-ing great. I have the ability to save Tom but I have no idea how to do it."

"Or if he'll even let you," I mumbled without thinking.

Arabella looked at me in question then her phone rang, making her jump. I glanced at the screen. It was Eve. My heart dropped. I had told her only to call if…

"Eve, what's happening?" Arabella answered, panic in her voice.

I could hear my sister on the other end. "Tom's okay. I'm sorry. I know I wasn't supposed to call but I'm going crazy here. Victor isn't answering his texts. What happened? When will you be back?"

A twinge of guilt for tossing my phone crossed my mind. I let out a breath and turned out their conversation. We still had time to save Tom but how was I supposed to protect Arabella from Seraphine? I met Rowan's eyes in the rear-view mirror again and I knew he was thinking the same thing.

* * *

The highway sign indicated our exit was next. Most of the drive had been quiet. Arabella had slept off and on. When she was awake, she asked more questions to Rowan who only had a few answers. Otherwise, she was on her phone with Eve and Acacia.

Rowan cleared his throat as I took the off-ramp. "Ara, we had a nice head start but we can't stay here long."

"What do you mean?"

"Seraphine is not going to forgive and forget. She's going to track you down and kill you," I explained.

Arabella put her head in her hands. "I just want my old life back."

Her words made my chest tight. She wanted to get married, work a job she loved, have kids, eat too much ice cream, and visit her family on the weekends. I stole all that away from her. She didn't deserve any of this. No wonder she hated me.

"Want or not. You've got a price on your head. Seraphine has dozens of reborn, and who knows how many living vampires who have sworn an oath. All of them will be wanting to win her favor by taking you out. We have two," Rowan explained.

"She doesn't know me. Surely it will take a while for them to find us."

My expression stopped her words. "Seraphine knows everything about me, and by proxy a lot about you."

"How long do we have?"

Rowan shook his head. "Today, maybe a little more but unless we travel by coffin, Victor and I are a liability during the day."

I parked near the hospital's main entrance, scanning the faces for any recognition of Seraphine's people. Most were huddled in coats and scarves hurrying on their way. Rowan let himself out the back. I turned off the car and reached for the door handle. Arabella put her hand on my arm. I looked back at her sad expression.

"Don't tell him."

I knew exactly what she meant. She didn't want Tom to know. Arabella didn't understand what she was and needed time to figure it out. Time, we didn't have.

I put my hand over hers. "He deserves to know what you are."

She pulled her hand free and shook her head. "Not yet. Maybe he'll recover and…"

"And what, you'll get married and live happily ever after? Don't you think he'll wonder why Rowan and I suddenly follow you everywhere. Or why you never age?"

Her phone buzzed in her lap. It was Eve. She glanced at the message then got out of the car without another word. I wanted so badly to go along with her plea but it wasn't something she could hide forever. Tom would have to change his mind about immortality before he knew. I could at least give her that.

Arabella was already inside when I met Rowan at the back of the car. He was looking down at his cream-colored shirt. Red-brown specks dotted across this chest. I glanced at my own but it was dark enough to mostly hide the blood stains. Eve would notice and I wasn't ready to have that conversation.

"You can borrow something of mine," I offered, grabbing my duffle.

I pulled out my bag and found us both new shirts. They were too casual for the rest of our attire but would have to do until I could get back to Eve's or until we left Montana all together. Rowan was right; we couldn't stay. Seraphine would burn this place to the ground until she got what she wanted.

Eve was standing outside Tom's room when we approached. She hugged me then Rowan for a bit longer than I liked. I opened my mouth to ask for an update when I heard Tom's voice. It was low and raspy but he was talking.

"He's getting better." Eve's voice wavered when she spoke. "They removed the ventilator a couple hours ago."

"Eve, Love. I would kill for some coffee." Rowan put his arm around her and steered her toward the elevators.

Appreciating Rowan's attempt to give me a minute of privacy, I stepped close and listened to Tom and Arabella's conversation. As much as I'd tried to mend our relationship, it was clear Tom still didn't trust me.

"I don't understand why you would go anywhere with Victor," Tom rasped. "What was he trying to get you to do?"

"It doesn't matter anymore. You're going to be okay and I'm here with you now." Arabella's calm voice surprised me, as she was never good at hiding her emotions.

"Are you really?" Tom asked accusingly.

Not only did my brother not trust me, but he also clearly didn't fully trust her either. Maybe that explained their extended engagement. I couldn't listen to him anymore. Arabella was hurting on so many levels. He didn't need to add to it.

"Hey, baby brother. You look better," I said as I walked to the end of his bed.

He actually looked worse. His hair was limp from fever and his lips still held a blue tinge. The oxygen tube didn't seem to be helping his breathing since it was irregular and harsh. He coughed for what seemed like forever, then closed his eyes and lay his head back.

Arabella's eyes held unshed tears as she stood. "I'm going to get some coffee too. I'll be right back."

Tom just nodded and kept his eyes closed. She silently pleaded for me to keep her secret and I would. For now.

As soon as she closed the door, I slapped Tom's foot. "What the hell is wrong with you?"

Tom opened his eyes and glared at me. "I know where you took her and why."

"I was trying to save your life, you ungrateful bastard."

Tom's laugh was harsh. "Indentured servitude and hiding in the shadows? That's not a life, Victor. That's purgatory."

I paced and ran my fingers through my hair. "When you have a choice, you would ignore it and just give everything up? You would be so selfish and leave her instead?"

Tom held my gaze. "Isn't that what you want? Wouldn't that make it easier for you?"

"Goddammit! This isn't about me. I did this for you."

"And?"

I held his stare for a heartbeat then answered. "And I did it for Arabellla. Losing you would have destroyed her. I had to do something." I sighed and turned away. "I love you, Tom, but you're an idiot. Giving up a few things to have the chance to be with someone who loves you unconditionally forever shouldn't be a difficult choice."

Tom coughed again so I turned back. "You're my brother, or you were, but I won't be a monster, Victor. What you are now isn't natural. People aren't meant to live forever. You're only supposed to get one shot at life. That's what makes it so special. When it's my time, I'll go. I'm not clinging to something that isn't real."

I knelt by his bed. "But it *is* real. I am still your brother. If I've changed, it's for the better. Don't dismiss this. You're making the biggest mistake of your life."

"I'm tired, Victor." Tom closed his eyes again. "Thanks for bringing her back to me."

Chapter Eighteen

When I wrenched the door open, I hadn't expected Arabella to still be standing there. Her expression told me she'd heard everything. I should have never taken her to Seraphine. I should have left them all alone. Tom wasn't the selfish one. That had always been me.

She shook her head and wiped her cheeks. "You don't have to say anything. I heard what I needed."

Rowan rushed Eve down the hall in our direction. "Time to go."

"But you just got here." Eve looked between the three of us.

I pulled Arabella's bag from her arm and rummaged through until I felt the pistol. Turning my body to block the nurse's station, I pressed it into Eve's hand.

"Unless it's Tom's doctor, aim for the head." Eve's eyes bulged and she tried to push the gun back to me. "Listen to me. You need to protect Tom and yourself. We'll protect Arabella. Eve, please."

Rowan had Arabella by the arm and was motioning with his other hand to get moving. Eve's confused and terrified eyes bounced between us trying to understand what was happening.

Arabella pulled her phone from her back pocket and handed it to Eve. "Tell Tom I'm sorry. I'll text you soon. Don't turn it off."

The elevator chimed and we ran. Two shots rang out followed by a door slam. Hopefully, that was Eve locking herself in Tom's room. She shouldn't be part of this but Seraphine wouldn't let anyone Arabella or I loved survive. That was not her MO.

The idiots who were chasing us didn't think to leave anyone by the car so that was our first win. We jumped in and I took off heading toward Arabella's parents' house. It took her a minute to put two and two together.

There weren't any cars when we pulled in the driveway but the front door was open. Arabella bolted for the house before Rowan or I could get out. We hurried after her.

"Acacia! Are you here?" Arabella shouted followed by a gut-wrenching scream.

I found them in the kitchen. Arabella was holding Acacia in her arms crying "no" over and over. Acacia was covered in blood and one arm was at an unnatural angle. When she coughed, blood poured from her lips.

"Please, please, how do I save her?" Arabella wailed.

Rowan knelt by them and spoke softly. "You know what to do. You were born to do this."

Acacia's eyes were wild and she clutched Arabella's shirt with her good hand. I could hear her heart beginning to stutter. It was now or never.

"Acacia, listen to me. I need you to do this." Arabella bit her wrist so blood welled then she pressed it against her sister's lips. "I won't ever ask you to do anything you don't want but please promise me you will."

Her sister's eyes closed and she drank. After a few pulls, she locked eyes with Arabella and nodded her head. Rowan got up and started checking the rest of the house. Reluctantly, I joined him.

I found him in Acacia's room with a black skull duffle bag in his hand. "Grab some clothes. She'll want to change later."

"How do you know she will…" I couldn't finish my thought.

Rowan gave me a light punch to the arm. "I need you to hold it together, mate. It'll work. Just grab some clothes and that hair brush over there."

Arabella was rocking a lifeless Acacia against her chest when we came back to the kitchen. Her eyes stared ahead at nothing and she pleaded to God under her breath. There was no sign of any change but I knew the process wasn't immediate. I went to the phone on the wall and scanned the printed list for their dad's cell. He picked up on the second ring.

"Mr. Simon. This is Victor River."

"Why the hell are *you* at my house in the middle of the night?" he answered.

"Mr. Simon, your daughters are fine. Get your wife and leave town now. Arabella will be in touch. Do not come home." I hung up before he could respond.

Rowan was trying to gently extract Acacia from Arabella but she wouldn't let go. "We can't stay here, Ara. Your sister's coming with us. She's going to be okay."

Arabella looked at me for confirmation then carefully transferred Acacia to Rowan. He picked her up and headed outside. I slung Acacia's bag over my shoulder and offered my hand to help her up. Instead, she looked at the blood that covered her hands and clothes.

"I don't think I can do this," she whispered.

I knelt down beside her. "Arabella, if anyone can do this, it's you. We need to leave or you just saved your sister for nothing."

At this, her head shot up and she locked eyes with me. "Take me home."

"I don't think that's a good idea. If they've already been here…"

"Take me home." She stood without my help and walked to the door then turned back. "Then we're going to kill that bitch."

* * *

The night was rushing along and we were running out of time. Arabella's bungalow was dark when we approached with no signs of movement inside or out. A streetlight shone on the snow blanketed park next door, lighting up the area and significantly reducing the chances of anyone sneaking up on us. Rowan got out and made a quick sweep of the house then gave the all-clear from the open front doorway.

"I'll be right back. I just need a few things."

I sat in the driver's seat and counted the seconds until they returned. In the quiet, I strained to hear any movement from Acacia. Nothing yet. Seraphine had pushed the wrong button, or in our case, the right one. Arabella wouldn't have gone along with murder without a shove and hurting her family was the only shove I knew that would get her onboard.

Arabella came out of the house with two bags. Rowan was a few steps behind and pulled the front door closed behind him. As soon as the connection was made, the windows exploded from the inside out. They both ducked automatically and hurried toward the car. Flames erupted and quickly engulfed the little house.

Rowan put one of the bags in the back and Arabella kept the other up front with her. She reached in and pulled out a much larger handgun than the one she'd left with Eve. With a flick, she released and checked the full clip then pulled back on the slide.

Without a backward glance at her burning home, she said, "Daylight is in a few hours. Stop at an ATM, then we're headed south."

Chapter Nineteen

We headed east then turned south a little less than an hour outside of town. Clearly Arabella had a destination in mind, which was good because we were chasing the sun. We now had three reborn and only two caskets. We needed someplace to stay soon.

When we turned into the little tourist town, I followed Arabella's directions to a group of cabins. When we pulled up to the first, a lighted sign blinked "Registration". I looked around and remembered that I was the only one not covered in blood.

"Ask for cabin eight," Arabella instructed.

I got out and made my way to the cabin. It was open and there was a little bell on the counter. I picked it up and gave it a shake. A deep bark sounded immediately after and I considered leaving, having never considered myself much of a dog person.

"I'm coming. I'm coming," a woman's voice sounded.

A little old lady with a gray bun and a very large black dog came around the corner. He gave me a sniff then sat down near my feet.

"Hi. I'm interested in renting cabin eight."

The woman gave me a once over then put on her readers. "How many in your party?"

"Three. I mean four. Sorry, it's been a long night."

"Uh-huh," she mumbled and began filling out a paper card. "Car?"

"Black Jaguar."

She gave me an impressed look and went back to the card. "Last name?"

I hesitated. We were off the main road but I didn't want any of Seraphine's flunkies to track us so I used my mother's maiden name. "Morrelli."

"There's a fifty-dollar deposit that will stay on your card until after our cleaning service is done. It's one-seventeen a night. How many nights?"

"Two." I pulled out my wallet and handed her six hundred dollar bills and let my persuasion slide into my next words. "I lost my credit card so I hope an extra deposit will make up for it."

She whipped out a marker and swiped each bill then held it up to the light. Apparently large bills are common in this town, as were fake ones.

"Cash always works, son." She pushed the money into her robe pocket then pulled a fish shaped key ring off the wall and handed it to me. "Cabin eight is on your left, just follow the road to the end. It'll be chilly but there's a wood stove and plenty of firewood out back."

I was thankful for the seclusion and the little dark we had left once Rowan told me we'd be bringing Acacia inside in the coffin. Damn, these things were heavy. No wonder he left them in the car. Arabella held the door but her eyes never left the glossy black surface.

Once it was safely tucked along the far wall, Rowan went outside to grab some firewood. Arabella headed to the bathroom. The two-room cabin held two Queen beds, a small kitchenette, and a sturdy looking sofa and armchair. A woodstove sat between them. The curtains had light shielding but not as much as we would need.

Rowan appeared with an armload of firewood then hurried back to the car. It took me a moment to comprehend the purpose of the double thickness aluminum foil and roll of duct tape. Once he pulled back the first set of curtains, it was clear he'd had to deal with less than perfect accommodations before. We worked quickly to cover all the windows in the main room.

The windows were blocked and fire was going by the time Arabella exited the bathroom. She'd taken a bath and changed her clothes. The cabin must come with toiletries because she smelled different than normal.

"How long before she wakes up?" she asked, gesturing to the coffin. "And do we know this will work since she only took my blood once?"

Rowan had removed his shirt and used a bottle of water to wash himself outside just before the sun hit the horizon. He was now reclining on the bed furthest from the window, despite the shielding. Considering how many times he'd saved our asses in the last two days, I didn't complain.

"She'll wake when the sun goes down. The transformation is not about the amount of shared blood, it's about the intention. You want your sister to live, so she will," he said then quickly added, "we should sleep in shifts."

She nodded, put her gun in her lap, and sat near the front door. "I'll keep the fire going."

I wanted to say something, anything, to take her mind off of, well everything but I had no words to give. Instead, I went to the bathroom to wash my hands and face. When I turned to leave, I saw Arabella's engagement ring sitting on the soap dish in the tub. Blood was stuck in the setting.

I plugged the sink and filled it with water as hot as I could get it then rubbed the ring clean. As I looked at its simplicity, it made me think of the necklace in my pocket. I pulled it out and held them side by side. They were opposing beauties. One so simple, one so elaborate. Both for someone more special than either of us could have ever realized.

A soft knock sounded and Arabella peeked in. She saw the ring in my left hand and gave me a sad smile then focused on the necklace in the other. I closed my right hand and held out the left, desperately wanting her to not take it.

"I wonder if Tom will ever forgive me for leaving again." She slipped the ring on and moved to leave then stepped in and shut the door. "That wasn't the present you were going to give me for Christmas, was it?"

I opened my hand again. "No. That was cocoa and cinnamon tequila."

She sat on the edge of the tub. "I could use some of that right now."

"You and me both," I agreed.

She rested her elbows on her knees. "Did I do the right thing? With Acacia, I mean. I keep thinking about what Tom said. What if I just damned my sister? I didn't give her a choice."

I squatted down in front of her. “You saved your sister. She may not have the life she thought she would but she will have one, and she’ll have you.”

Arabella chewed her lip and nodded in thought. “We can’t go back, Victor. I’ll never forget what you did to me. But I’m in uncharted waters here and I need your help.”

“Wow. Did that hurt?”

“Ha ha. I can ask for help when I need it.” Arabella’s put-out look changed to deadly serious. “Show me I can trust you.”

* * *

I woke up to slow knocking and was momentarily disoriented. The room was dim in the twilight dusk coming from the open bathroom door. Rowan was still passed out on his stomach and Arabella was asleep slumped in the armchair. So much for sleeping in shifts. The banging sounded again.

Arabella jumped upright and pulled open the coffin. Acacia sat up and looked around.

“I had the weirdest dream.” She looked around and down to where she was sitting then covered her mouth with her hands. “Am I *in* a coffin?”

Arabella hugged her sister tightly while both crying and laughing. “Yes, you are in a coffin. I finally found a perfect bed for my Goth sister.”

Rowan pushed himself upright and yawned. “Good evening, Beautiful. A bit hungry, are we?”

Acacia moved her hand to her throat and swallowed hard. I had forgotten about the intense thirst after rebirth. She would need human blood soon or she'd be uncontrollable. That was the last thing we needed to deal with right now.

Arabella seemed to catch on but quickly changed the subject. "Let's get you cleaned up."

She helped Acacia to the bathroom and shut the door. I could hear their voices rise and fall as Arabella explained what happened. After a good amount of yelling and shushing, their voices fell to a full murmur. This little town better have a bar. I needed a drink.

"Well, Victor, we've gotten ourselves into quite a pickle." Rowan looked at his blood stained shirt then tossed it back on the floor. "Guess I'm hitting the gift shop then off to find some dinner?"

"About that…" I started.

Rowan pointed at the bathroom. "That little girl in there is going to need blood and soon or she's not going to be very pleasant."

"Believe me, I remember. We're all going to need it but somehow I don't think Arabella is going to be thrilled with how we used to do things."

Rowan's brow wrinkled then realization hit. "Well, that complicates things, or uncomplicates them. Hiding the bodies was always the hard part. I can go easy. Can't promise that for the newbie though."

When the girls emerged, Acacia was clean and dressed in her usual black. Her eyes flicked to mine then Rowans then back to her sister. "Where are we exactly?"

"Remember the cabin Mom and Dad used to take us to when we went hunting for sapphires?"

"Oh yeah. I knew it looked familiar but why are they here?"

Rowan put his arm around her shoulders. "We have a very long drive ahead of us and apparently, my radio sucks, so we will answer all your questions on the road. But first, let's go get you some dinner."

"Rowan, I…" Arabella started.

I interrupted her. "This is all part of rebirth. We'll take care of her. Trust me."

Using her words against her was cruel but we had to start somewhere.

* * *

We walked from the cabin, which turned out to be farther than planned but Rowan's car is too recognizable. This was not a high-end tourist town, more of a blue-collar vacation destination. The bar was just as seedy as I imagined it would be. There was only one in town and the floor was covered in peanut shells. It took everything I had to not walk right back out. The crazy thing was no one else even batted an eye.

Rowan, donning his newly acquired pink moose print shirt, headed straight to the bar while the girls found a booth in the back corner. I joined my friend at the bar. The bartender had on a dingy white apron and an even dingier towel slung over his shoulder. As soon as I touched the counter, I wished I hadn't.

"Two whiskeys and two ginger ales," Rowan ordered. "You having anything, mate?"

"Any chance you have cinnamon tequila?" I asked but he shook his head. "I'll take a bottle of whatever red wine you have."

I turned my back to the bar and scanned the meager crowd. Other than a couple twenty-something meatheads, everyone looked like a local. An old cowboy dozed at the bar. A group of middle-aged men in overalls watched football and sipped beer. A couple sat hand in hand near the door with brightly colored cocktails. Said meatheads kept looking at my girls and whispering.

Rowan slapped me on the shoulder. "Lower those hackles, mate. Acacia can take them both. We, on the other hand, will have to work for our meals."

I turned back to the bar and noticed a food menu on a white board. "Send over a plate of the nachos, extra jalapenos."

Rowan managed to carry over all four glasses so I grabbed my bottle and tried not to look too closely at the wine glass. At least none of us had to worry about food poisoning. Acacia was holding Arabella's hands across the table when we sat.

"How are you feeling?" Arabella asked after Acacia took a sip of her ginger ale and grimaced.

"Weird. I can't really describe it but I feel like everything is overwhelming, even my own skin. Nothing looks or tastes like it should."

"You'll get used to that. It also fades a bit but your senses are a bit more active than before," I explained.

Rowan tossed back one whiskey then looked at Acacia. "You should ask those wrestle-star wannabes to play darts."

Acacia glanced over at the guys then quickly looked away. "I don't think so."

Rowan took a sip of his second whiskey. "You have to eat."

Arabella sat back and scanned the room. It was like watching her work. She was breaking down every part of the room and everyone in it. I could almost see her checking things off in her head.

"I think we should go somewhere else," she said as the nachos arrived. "Soon. We should go someplace else soon."

I hid a chuckle as she snagged a cheese covered chip. Acacia reached for the plate too but Rowan intercepted her hand. Apparently, Arabella had skipped a few details. Food was a tough one to give up and those nachos looked pretty good.

"Let's find something on that jukebox and you give me a dance. I have an idea." Rowan winked at me as he pulled Acacia from the booth.

I didn't like the sound of that but he hadn't steered us wrong yet. They stayed in my peripheral vision and I kept Arabella quiet company. The wine wasn't terrible either. Without the pressure of impending death, this might have been an okay evening. A slap rang out and my eyes jerked to Acacia and Rowan.

"Pervert!" Acacia yelled then stomped over to the bar, two seats away from her targets.

"Victor, I don't know if I'm okay with this. Those guys are twice her size."

"She's got back up but she's not going to need it."

Meathead One slid over so he was right next to Acacia and offered his hand. She looked at it for a moment then took it and shared her name. The other crossed his arms and stared menacingly at Rowan who was sulking by the jukebox. A shot quickly appeared before Acacia.

"I can't watch this." Arabella picked up Rowan's remaining whiskey and tipped it back.

"You want another?" I asked, expecting a snarky comeback but she just nodded.

When I made it to the bar, I purposely stood next to Acacia and her new friends so I could eavesdrop and break necks if necessary.

"Is there anything fun to do around here? I'm stuck out here with my sister and her stupid friends." Acacia played with her drink. "So boring."

She was good. No wonder Arabella was uneasy. This was not the first time Acacia had picked up someone in a bar.

"Two more whiskeys," I ordered.

"Yeah. We can show you a good time. Your sister won't mind if we steal you away?" Meathead One replied.

"No way. She can't wait to have some alone time with this fun sucker."

I turned away from the threesome and tried to hide my smile. Even under pressure and recovering from rebirth, she still knew how to slide one between the ribs. That little twerp was growing on me.

The lurker picked up Acacia and set her gently on her feet. Arabella was right, he was more than double her weight and head and shoulders taller. She giggled and followed them outside. Rowan waited about ten seconds then followed.

Arabella craned her neck. "I should go after her."

I put the shot in front of her. "Rowan won't let anything happen. She needs this. Next time won't be so bad but the first is not something you want to see. Here's to the newest addition of your undead army."

She had picked up the shot glass but put it back down at my words. I clicked my glass to hers and lifted it in encouragement.

"It's hard not to hate you," she said, then tossed back her shot followed by a big swig of ginger ale.

Chapter Twenty

Once the nachos were gone, Arabella stood. "Let's see if the gas station has prepaid phones. I'm sure Eve and my mom are losing their minds. Plus, I forgot toothpaste."

It was a good excuse for her to get outside but she was right. We needed to check in with Eve. I'd been worried about her too. Seraphine's people would chase us first but if they got stuck, they would put pressure on our loved ones. Acacia was proof of that.

Arabella tried to be nonchalant while looking for Acacia as we made our way down the street. She was also a bit stumbly from the drinks and I couldn't help but laugh.

"What?" she snapped.

"It's not like Rowan is going to let her start feeding on Main Street. Stop worrying. They'll meet us back at the cabin."

She was quiet for a block or so. "What about you?"

"I'm not worried about them."

"No. Don't you need, well, you know?"

I stopped walking and met her gaze. "Yes, but I'm not leaving you alone. Once you are safely back with Rowan, I'll step out for a bit."

The gas station was shockingly well stocked with everything from candy, soda, movies, electronics, clothing, and even hunting gear. That's Montana for you. While Arabella looked at the phones, I flipped through the t-shirts without really looking. Eventually Rowan and I would need more clothes, but I wasn't going to wear something with a picture of a deer on it.

Arabella took two phones to the register and I placed two large water bottles and a tube of toothpaste next to them. She gave me a small smile. The cashier rang us up at sloth speed, no emotion, and slower than cold tar. I resisted the urge to snap her neck.

We'd made it back to the cabin road before I spoke again. "We're going to need a different vehicle. There's not really enough room unless we plan on stopping each morning."

"I was wondering about that." Arabella started but screeching tires cut her off.

A panel van jumped the curb and gunned it. Out of instinct, Arabella shoved me out of the way and took the full impact. Her body flipped over the vehicle and landed face down in the road. I was supposed to be protecting her dammit!

The reverse lights lit and the van started backing as if to run over her body. I launched myself in her direction and was able to pull her aside just in time. Through the windshield I could see one of Seraphine's bodyguards; the guy I recognized at the big house. His gapped tooth grin reflected in the dash lights and he put the car in drive again.

Rowan and Acacia must have caught up with us because he wrenched the door open and pulled the guy out of the van. It continued to roll in our direction. I covered Arabella and braced for impact, which never came. The headlights stopped inches away and blinded me.

The engine and lights cut off then Acacia jumped out and yelled, "Arabella! Are you okay?"

I gently moved to assess her injuries. Any regular person would probably be dead. Arabella was just knocked out. The left side of her body was covered in scrapes and she had a gash on her forehead.

"Help me get her into the van."

Acacia scrambled to open the back. I could hear Rowan continuing to fight with the driver. Another sharp punch and the noise silenced. When I turned, he was straddling the now unconscious man, chest heaving with exertion.

"I've always wanted to give this guy a beat down. I bloody hate this fucker."

Rowan pulled the man's limp body toward the van. I stepped between him and the vehicle. No way was he going in the back with Arabella.

"Listen, I'd love to pull this arsehole's head off right here but we're a bit exposed and we need answers. Get out of the way or carry him back yourself."

He was right. We needed to know how this guy found us and if he was alone. I motioned for Acacia to pull Arabella all the way in the van. Rowan and I tossed the body in unceremoniously after her.

Due to Christmas, or maybe it was just the off season, we were the only cabin tenants. I'm sure that old woman saw every move we made but there weren't any other prying eyes. The black dog was laying on the porch of the first cabin and lifted his head as we drove by.

When we pulled the van behind cabin eight, Rowan pushed the bodyguard out of the van, letting him bounce off the ground. I helped Acacia carefully move Arabella from the van to the couch. She still hadn't woken up.

"Is she going to be okay?" Acacia asked, brushing some hair out of her sister's face and looking more closely at the cut on her forehead.

"She'll be fine. Go help Rowan." I tried to keep my voice calm then let some persuasion slide in. "I'll take care of her. Just go."

Acacia sat back on her heels. "You know I can tell when you try that shit, right? It's like I feel a shove in my brain. Too bad for you, I can shove back."

She stood and left the cabin. I'd never met a person who could resist my persuasion abilities. I guess if anyone was stubborn enough, it was Acacia. Seems like the little sister was more than I realized too.

Arabella took a deep breath then groaned. Her hands went to her ribs on her left side. Now that she was laying down, I could see her side was dented inward. The impact must have broken a few ribs.

"Rowan and I are supposed to be protecting you, remember? No more throwing yourself into harm's way."

"Force of habit." She exhaled then winced. "Did we win?"

"You're still alive. So, yes in a manner of speaking, we won."

"I'm not going to heal on my own, am I?" Her eyes were still closed but worry crinkled her forehead.

"You've got Rowan and me for that too."

Her eyes opened and focused on me. She didn't want to be dependent on anyone, especially me. Our trust was still too fragile. So, like an idiot, I attempted a joke.

"Next time you let me get hit by the car and you won't have to take my blood."

She laughed then gasped. "I hate you so much right now."

"I would expect nothing less."

* * *

Arabella excused herself to the bathroom after taking my blood. I was grateful because I needed a minute alone. While she seemed to be less and less affected by my blood, every time seemed more intense for me. I needed to talk to Rowan but it would have to wait since I heard voices outside the cabin.

"I ain't telling you shit!"

A punch followed. "Why are you still listening to that spoiled little brat? What has she done for you lately?"

I stepped outside and took a deep breath. Acacia sat in the driver's seat of the van watching through the open side panel as Rowan interrogated the bodyguard. She looked both mildly amused and horrified. Rowan definitely had a way with people.

"Traitor. She's the reason you're alive," he spat.

"Okay, let's try this. Who else is with you? How did you find us?"

"Fuck off!" he said then spit in Rowan's face.

Rowan wiped his cheek with the back of his hand then turned to me. "I don't think he feels like sharing. Let's get it over with and tie him up at the east side of the rise there. The sun will be coming up soon."

The bodyguard began to struggle harder in panic. "Rowan, what's come over you, man? Why are you throwing this all away?"

Rowan adjusted his stance and put his hands on the other's shoulders. "Freedom, you wanker."

With a quick twist, Rowan broke the guy's neck. I heard Acacia gasp. She needed to be brought up to speed quickly. We couldn't stay another day, we needed to pack up and leave now, even as dawn approached.

Rowan and I carried the body to the edge of the trees. There was a break facing east. I had no idea my friend was so cold hearted. The man wasn't forever dead yet. He'd recover in time but not with the sun bath he was about to receive. Once again, I was glad Rowan was on my side.

When we made it back to the cabin, Arabella and Acacia were loading the second coffin into the back of the van. We quickly moved our few belongings in as well. Looks like our vehicle problem solved itself. The van was windowless except for the windshield plus driver and passenger doors. If two of us stayed in the coffins, another could be in the very back and still be protected from sunlight.

A thought crossed my mind and I quickly walked up to cabin one. The dog was still laying on the porch. I reach down to give him a scratch between the ears. He made a happy sound and laid back down. I opened the door to find the old woman sitting in a recliner with a romance novel.

We didn't really have time for pleasantries so I let persuasion saturate my words. "We're going to leave the Jag here, in your shop out back. Don't tell anyone we were here or what you saw."

Her words were slow as she nodded. "What I saw."

I went around the desk and pocketed the card with my information. "Or about this," I whispered in her ear and bit her neck.

The warm blood filled my mouth and I had to focus on not draining her dry. She'd have a headache when she woke up but would keep her promise.

Chapter Twenty-One

"Mom. No, Mom. We're both fine. No, she's asleep. Mom, stop. Could you just-" Arabella's voice rose with every word. "Mom, I need you to listen to me!"

We hit the rumble strips and my head began to clear. Soft light coming through the windshield told me the sun had just gone down. I had offered to sleep in the back of the van and let Rowan and Acacia have the more comfortable accommodations. The hard floor made me regret that decision now.

Arabella held the phone away from her ear as her mom continued to yell. I climbed into the passenger seat and she gave me an exasperated look. Somehow, the prepaid cell phones had survived our little traffic accident last night.

"If you don't stop screaming at me, I'm going to hang up!" Arabella yelled at the phone.

After a moment of silence, she put the phone back to her ear. "I need you to call the venue and caterer to tell them we need to postpone."

The yelling started again and I heard the plastic crack as Arabella's grip tightened. When the tirade stopped, Arabella tried again. "Because Tom's still in the hospital and I'm out of state. No, I don't know when I'll be back. Just call them."

When the voice on the other end increased in pitch again, Arabella rolled down the window and tossed the phone out. I would have laughed if her words hadn't struck a chord. She wanted to postpone, not cancel the wedding. Instead, I let out a slow breath and focused on the scenery. We were on a two-lane highway surrounded by forest.

"Sorry you had to hear that. I called my dad but she grabbed the phone. I knew she'd go ballistic, which is why I called him. They're staying in Coeur d'Alene so they should be safe for now." She pushed her hair back and gave me a sideways glance. "Were you okay back there? I know I drive a bit aggressively."

"That's the understatement of the year, but it was fine." I tried to keep my answer light because I wasn't sure how she'd respond to my next question. "Did you talk to Eve?"

Arabella nodded and continued to stare forward at the road. Not a good conversation then. Emotions flitted across her face and she drove. She was supposed to be preparing for a wedding. Instead, I was leading us toward what could be our deaths.

"We're almost to Boise," Arabella said with a roll of her shoulders.

She needed a break, which gave me an idea. "We've been rather hard on what little clothing we have. It would be a good idea to pick up a few things."

Arabella followed the signs to the outlet mall and parked. She hopped out and stretched, which was impressive considering she was run over last night. That thought brought a frown to my face. I still needed to talk to Rowan about how her blood affected me. And even more, about the fact that I wasn't sure I was ever going to let her take anyone else's.

I knocked on the coffins and got out myself. The parking lot was surprisingly full of after Christmas shoppers. I scanned cars and faces for anyone I recognized. Seraphine's people could be anywhere.

Rowan and Acacia joined us and we headed inside. The girls headed into a store right away and I motioned for Rowan to follow me farther down the walkway.

"I applaud your confidence, bruv, but I don't think we should leave them alone." Rowan's eyes followed the girls.

"I have a few questions that I'd rather not share with company. We can give them a few minutes."

Rowan shrugged and took a seat on one of the metal benches just outside the store, making it clear he wasn't going far.

"Do we actually have a plan? You know Seraphine is going to be surrounded by reborn. She's not going to let us just waltz up to her."

Rowan watched a couple of middle-aged women walk by before answering. "You aren't really going to love my plan and I need your reactions to be genuine."

"What the fuck does that mean?" My voice carried and I forced myself to rein it in. "I am not going in blind."

"Have I steered you wrong yet?" Rowan slapped me on the back, which made me want to punch him in the face. "Listen, Seraphine isn't going to cancel her New Year's party for anything. That is our in. Plus, we have a secret weapon."

"Which is?" My patience was almost gone.

"Acacia, of course." He sat back and folded his hands behind his head. "If we can keep her rebirth from becoming common knowledge, she won't be seen as a threat."

I grimaced, remembering how I'd used Acacia to force Arabella's hand before. She was most definitely not going to be thrilled. That made me think of another question.

"Rowan, how did you know Acacia could be turned? I mean, she's a first generation and for all we knew was a living immortal too."

This time it was Rowan's turn to look uncomfortable. "Lucky guess, mate. Oh look, here come our girls now."

Acacia was eyeing me so I rearranged my features to a normal amount of annoyance, rather than complete shock. Rowan could have completely broken Arabella had the rebirth not occurred. He was playing with something he didn't understand. His confession reminded me of how little I actually knew about the man and how many secrets he held. However, he was correct on one part. He had not steered us wrong yet so for now, I'd let him keep pushing us forward.

"How do you ladies like parties?" Rowan asked, throwing his arm around Acacia's shoulder.

Arabella's cheeks turned pink and I knew she was about to lose it so I stepped in. "Seraphine hosts a New Year's Eve bash every year. It may be our chance to get close to her."

"And?" Arabella still looked ready to blow.

"And it's our best shot," Rowan answered. "It's a formal affair so at least we get to be fancy."

I forced myself not to strangle him. "I am not wearing an off the rack tux, Rowan. What are the odds that my house is still standing?"

Rowan grimaced. "Doubtful and if it is, it's probably rigged like Arabella's place."

A moment of sadness flickered across her face and Acacia looked between us in question. I'd forgotten she was otherwise occupied at the time. Arabella had stopped at the mall map and was scanning the stores.

"This one will have to do." She pointed at the name; it was not one I recognized.

Rowan nodded. "What about you lovely ladies?"

"We're covered," Arabella said flatly as she turned and walked away toward our destination.

Acacia freed herself from Rowan's arm and quickly caught up. "I thought I recognized that other bag in the van. Are you sure?"

Arabella continued walking for a few moments before replying. "There's a good chance I'm not going to need it anyway."

* * *

The store wasn't bad, but it wasn't great. The materials were cheap and the prices inflated. We were being helped by a high school kid who was more interested in flirting with Acacia than actually doing his job. I, for one, was grateful to be left alone.

Rowan was drawn to the wide lapels and ruffled shirts. His sense of fashion made me want to slap him. Considering his age, I'd give him a pass but after we got through this, he and I were going to have a chat.

Against my better judgment, Arabella was next door getting undergarments and leggings for both the girls. We needed to hurry or I wouldn't have let her out of my sight. Even so, I kept glancing out the door in hopes she'd appear.

The silk blend charcoal gray shirt was a brand I'd recognized. I'd yet to find pants that weren't polyester. This was going to be a nightmare but I could slum it for a good cause.

"So, are you from around here?" the teenage idiot asked Acacia.

Acacia caught my eye and I subtly shook my head. Her eyes roamed to Rowan who was busy sorting through plaid bow ties. She seemed genuinely bothered after her conversation with Arabella about the contents of the mystery bag.

"Arizona," she said with a light laugh.

"No," I said as Rowan walked toward me with an armload of colorful clothing.

"What? I just want to try a few things on." Rowan tried to catch the teen's attention then shrugged and headed to the dressing rooms.

I put a couple pairs of slacks over my arm and followed. We were alone and I wasn't sure when I would get the chance again. I could hear him shuffling around in the room next to mine.

"Rowan," I spoke softly but I knew he could hear me. "I think I have a problem."

"Bruv, you have so many. Where to start?"

I closed my eyes and imagined myself beating the crap out of my friend before continuing. "It's about Arabella."

"Most of them are."

I punched the wall between us, leaving a fist shaped dent. "I'm serious. I think there is something wrong with our binding. What her blood does to me and what happens when she takes mine is not… right."

Rowan stopped moving and I waited. "Most bindings are business dealings. Yours is decidedly not. You've got your entire self wrapped up in that girl."

I let out a breath. "That's an understatement."

"Exactly. As her clan of reborn grows, you're going to have to share." Rowan went back to trying on clothes.

Finally, I said out loud what I'd feared since I got my first taste of her blood back at Eve's condo. "I'm not sure that's going to happen."

I pulled on the first pair of slacks and frowned. They were awful. The next were tolerable and we were running out of time. I got redressed and stepped back into the hall.

Rowan took a few more minutes then joined me with the most hideous light blue tux pants and ruffled shirt I'd ever seen, an orange and navy plaid bow tie in his left hand. Knowing my luck, they'd have a matching jacket. I was going with standard black and wished I could convince him of the same but now wasn't the time for fashion advice.

He looked at me with the most serious expression I've even seen from him. "Victor, once Seraphine is dead, everything's going to change. Arabella is the key. Right now, you need to focus on keeping her safe. We can figure out the rest after."

Yeah, if after exists.

When I stepped out into the main store, Arabella was standing with Acacia holding two pink striped bags. She was laughing at something the idiot teen had said. For that one moment, the weight was lifted and her beauty struck me as it had the first time I laid eyes on her.

She glanced my way and her entire demeanor darkened. This was business to her. A job like any other. Right now, she was my entire world. When this was over, she'd walk away and I would have nothing left to live for.

Chapter Twenty-Two

Acacia sat in one of the open coffins as we drove. She'd been quiet since the mall. That wasn't really surprising. The rebirth process takes days, followed by weeks to fully wrap your head around the change. She hadn't had any warning or preparation. I felt sorry for the little twerp.

Arabella had been asleep next to her for hours. Rowan and I stayed in our own heads. The radio had been hit or miss as we traveled through the mountains. The occasional semi was our only company on the road.

"Where are we headed?" Acacia asked, pulling me from my personal pity party.

"Reno," Rowan answered, then checked his side mirror again. "I know some place safe we can stay."

This was news to me. He hadn't been very forthcoming after I caught him checking an old school flip phone. Other than stating that he'd bought it before we hit the bar, he played it off as no big deal. I noticed he was only texting one number that I didn't recognize. The language was not English, which also made me more than a little uncomfortable.

Acacia moved so she was sitting crossed legged just behind the front seats. It appeared she was finally ready to talk. Still, it took her another half an hour before she spoke.

"Arabella told me she turned me and that's why the people are chasing us. I didn't know she could do that, did you?" she asked me and when I shook my head she continued. "Of course, she's a frickin' living immortal! She's always been special, even though she can't see it. Why is she so sad though?"

I thought about that for a second. "Your sister has always wanted to be 'normal'. The more she tries, the more it slips from her grasp."

"So, Rowan, you're the guy Eve has a crush on." Acacia quickly switched topics. "You know she's my girlfriend, right?"

Rowan snuck a glance at her and laughed. "I can't control who falls in love with me but I promise you have nothing to worry about. Eve's not my type."

Now it was my turn to laugh. "Bull shit. I haven't met a woman alive who isn't your type."

"Bloody hilarious," was Rowan's deadpan reply. "Remember what I said about my previous sire's extracurriculars? Young women like Eve and you dear Acacia, are a bit too close to his preferred type. It makes me uncomfortable, like I'm a pedo too."

That made a lot of sense. While women followed Rowan like puppy dogs, he tended to lean toward older women, more like my mother's age or older. I guess he could give the middle-aged women an ego boost and he could get what he needed.

"Are you guys hungry all the time or is it just me?" Acacia flipped topics again.

"That fades but your body is going through a major change. You can eat when we get to Reno."

"Here's a weird thing maybe you can explain. Even when I can't see Arabella, I can feel where she is. Will that fade too?"

I looked at Rowan because I knew exactly what Acacia meant. It hadn't faded for me but I was relatively newly reborn as well. When she was too far, it was like my skin itched and there was a pressure in the back of my skull. That must have been why Montana was my first thought when I was put on sabbatical. Speaking of which, I was going to have to look for a new job if we survived this. California was too far away from her, no matter what life she chose.

"Not so much fade really, but you'll be able to tolerate it more as time goes on. Less like ants under your skin to more like when the feeling comes back after you hit your funny bone."

"Well, that sounds… awful. Hang on. Does that mean I have to live with her now?" She turned to me. "Does that mean *you* have to live with her now?"

Living arrangements had not crossed my mind. Arabella's house was destroyed and we couldn't all fit in Eve's condo. Eventually, we'd need to discuss what comes after our confrontation with Seraphine, or maybe not.

Rowan must have noticed my hesitation and changed the subject. "Wanna know some of the cool stuff about being a reborn immortal?"

He flipped off the headlights and pressed the pedal down. The van had more power than it appeared. It's previous owner obviously modified more than the interior. Rowan wove in and out of the trucks with ease.

"You can see better and farther. You're stronger, as long as you feed regularly. Death is difficult. There are only a handful of ways to permanently kill an immortal."

"Which are?" she asked.

I turned back to look at her. The gold of her irises glowed but not like Arabella's. They were more yellowish white while her sister's were like liquid gold. The memory triggered a deep need to see it again, and soon.

"Why? Are you planning on taking us out in our sleep?" Rowan joked. "Sunlight is the big one. It's very difficult to heal from even a small exposure but it takes a long time to actually die. Prolonged exposure to fire is a tough one to recover from too and most don't. Loss of your head is another. Lack of human blood won't actually kill you but too long without it and you'll lose yourself to madness."

I knew all this but I felt like he was holding back. "And?"

Rowan turned the headlights back on and slowed down. "Your living immortal can revoke your agreement."

"That's not funny," I said with a light laugh.

Rowan gave me a sad smile. He wasn't joking and his look told me that he was downright terrified. Seraphine wasn't his sire but he was bound to her. I could see in his eyes that he didn't plan on walking away from this. This was his redemption.

* * *

Arabella woke up when Rowan turned off the van. Clearly stress sleep was still her thing. We were in a subdivision somewhere in central Reno. The Bungalow style houses looked identical other than the bright colors that alternated from one house to the next.

When we piled out, a man opened the door. He was utterly forgettable, nothing about him stood out. Everything about him was tan from his boring haircut to his skin, he was even wearing khaki shorts. Rowan hurried ahead of us and shook the man's hand.

"Guys, this is Joseph. Joseph, this is Victor, Acacia, and," he paused, "Arabella."

I didn't like how he hesitated before saying her name, like it held some special meaning. Joseph nodded at each of us then headed back inside. The girls looked as confused as me.

"Rowan, is this guy okay?" I asked.

Rowan smiled. "Yeah, we go way back. He's not much of a talker but he's cool. We can stay here until New Year's. Grab your bags. I'm going to pull the van in the garage."

The inside of the house looked like a model home. No signs of personalization or uniqueness. Earthy tones were everywhere I looked, but the windows… That's when I started to notice a difference. This was a safe house, but not one of Seraphine's. My blood ran cold. We'd entered the dwelling of another clan.

Joseph ushered the girls upstairs while I waited for Rowan. Everything about this felt wrong but once again we were fighting sunrise. The floor creaked as the trio moved about on the second floor. What was taking Rowan so long?

Joseph descended the stairs and we sized each other up. We stood eye to eye when he was on the last step. His voice was not at all what I expected, a slow deep bass with what felt like a touch of my own persuasion. I liked him even less.

"I can tell you do not want to be here. Worry not, Victor. The enemy of my enemy is my friend."

Rowan entered at that moment with his own backpack. We'd each bought a few sets of clothes at the mall. The girls seemed to need some time somewhat alone and it gave us all a few moments of normalcy.

"Joseph, any of the regulars available tonight? It's been a long trip."

Joseph nodded and walked into the kitchen. He handed a stack of paper to-go menus to Rowan who in turn gave them to me.

"For the girls," Rowan said with a knowing look.

I glanced at the menus then headed upstairs. Despite his reassurance, Rowan only somewhat trusted this guy. Acacia was our only trump card. We needed to keep her rebirth a secret, even from someone helping us. Hopefully Joseph hadn't noticed her lack of heartbeat.

I could hear the girls' low voices and I considered eavesdropping but the floor creaked under my weight. Arabella's head popped out the door at the end. She stepped around the door and pulled it closed behind her. I held out the menus to her.

"Order something for two." I started to turn away, hoping she'd catch my drift.

"Victor, wait…" she started.

I kept my back turned, not ready to talk about anything else. "Everything's okay. We're safe here, for now."

Chapter Twenty-Three

I would never take a bed or shower for granted again. Despite my turmoiled brain, I was able to get some sleep. Acacia sharing a room with Arabella kept me from barging in and demanding something I knew she'd refuse. She was not mine. She may never be mine in the way I wanted. But Rowan was right, Arabella was the key.

My focus needed to be on the mission but I was still hung up on the fact we were in another clan's territory. Rowan himself warned me of how dangerous this was and told me Seraphine had taken out all the other living immortals in the US. So, how was it we were here? What else had he lied about? We were twenty-four hours from confronting Seraphine. I needed answers.

When I stepped out of my room and passed the bathroom, I thought I heard crying. My first thought was Acacia. The transition can be painful both mentally and physically. She was still literally a child. It wasn't fair.

As I listened more closely, the crying was muffled like someone was trying to not be heard. The "regulars" Rowan had referred to last night were humans who offered their blood to immortals, like groupies. We had been successful in getting one to Acacia without Joseph noticing but I was sure they had all left hours ago. That only left one other female who could be crying.

My heart ached as I listened to Arabella sob in the shower. The sound came in waves like she was trying to stop but couldn't. She was the strongest, most stubborn woman I had ever met. Everything in her life was wrong. Everything in her life was broken. And it was all my fault.

"She cries in her sleep too." Acacia's voice startled me.

I nodded and lowered my hand, which had moved to the bathroom doorknob on its own. Every fiber of my being wanted to make it right for her.

Acacia spoke again. "I want to make her pain stop too but I don't know how."

"How did you know what I was thinking?" I asked.

She gave me a look. "You're pretty easy to read."

"Let's give her some space. We need to talk to Rowan anyway."

We headed downstairs despite the pull I had to comfort Arabella. Joseph and Rowan were in the living room speaking in hushed voices.

"Thanks for the Chinese food, Joe," Acacia said as she folded her legs under herself to sit against the far wall.

He tilted his head in her direction. "You are most welcome but please, it is Joseph."

"Sure." She grabbed a photo book from the coffee table and started to flip through it.

I joined the men. Their conversation seemed to have ended. My discomfort with Rowan and the situation was growing. Joseph waited a few moments then rose and left the room.

"Rowan, what the fuck is going on?" I asked, attempting to keep my voice down despite my anger.

He sat back and regarded Acacia. "We have a day to recover and regroup. Everything is going to plan, mate. Stop worrying."

I ran my hand through my hair in frustration. "You told me Arabella's safety was paramount. I don't feel safe, which means she's definitely not safe."

Rowan sat forward and put his elbows on his knees. "You have to trust me. We are so close to finishing this. Don't fall apart on me now."

"Finishing what? I feel like this is so much more than switching alliances with you."

"I have a bit more at stake than you, mate." Rowan's anger surprised me. "We're going to do this and we're going to do it my way so you can have whatever fucked up version of happily ever after you want. All I need is for you to chill out and follow my lead."

My eyes flicked over to Acacia who was studying the art book with forced intensity as she tried not to listen to our argument.

"Fine." I gritted my teeth. "What *is* your lead?"

Rowan looked over my shoulder and smiled. "Arabella! You look like you slept well."

She looked perfect. There was no sign that she had been crying. She wore new sweatpants and a fitted t-shirt. Her hair was down and still wet from the shower. Her bare feet showed newly painted black toenails. I guess her and Acacia had some catching up time while I slept.

"Thanks." She smiled then her stomach rumbled. "Any chance I could get another to-go order?"

"Pizza and ice cream are already on their way." Joseph appeared at the doorway, making Acacia jump.

"Thanks, Joseph. I appreciate you letting us stay here." Arabella sounded genuinely grateful.

When he nodded his head in acknowledgment, it looked a little too much like a bow for my tastes. This was getting out of my control too quickly. I could almost feel her being pulled into a world she wasn't prepared for or even wanted. More importantly, I could feel her slipping further away from me.

Arabella sat next to Acacia but Rowan cleared his throat. "We need to talk about tomorrow."

Everyone moved so we were sitting around the central coffee table. Arabella across from me, next to Rowan, so Acacia reluctantly joined me on the love seat. The dark cloud seemed to have descended over us again. The moment of reprieve was over.

"The three of us are targets. Acacia is not. She's our in." Arabella opened her mouth to interrupt but Rowan put his hand on her knee with a look. "We need someone to get into the party and let us in a side entrance. There is no way we are walking through the front door. But I'm getting ahead of myself."

I rubbed my hand over my face afraid this was going to be another one of his long diatribes. My patience no longer existed and I was tired of being in the dark. What he said next made me see red.

"Arabella, if you will permit me to take some of your blood, my goal is to convince Seraphine that I have genuinely come back to her. If I'm lucky, I might be able to incapacitate her with your blood in my veins."

"Absolutely not!" I roared and jumped from my seat.

Arabella moved just as quickly and put herself between me and Rowan. "Victor, please." Her tone made me pause." Hear him out."

I sat down as Rowan continued. "The short version is we somehow manage to get on the grounds without being seen, Acacia enters the party alone without being stopped so she can let us in through the kitchen, and I incapacitate Seraphine while Victor and Arabella get into place in the master suite on the second floor. Once she is stunned, Arabella gets to use that hand cannon she so smartly retrieved from her house. Then all we have to do is get out of the house before Seraphine's devotees find us."

Arabella chewed her lip but wouldn't make eye contact with me. Actually, she hadn't made eye contact with me since I told her we were safe here. Had I already broken the fragile trust we'd just formed?

"Do you have a map of the house?" she asked.

"No, and there are no copies. Seraphine makes modifications constantly as a way to protect herself anyway. All I can give you is a direct path."

"All I have to do is go into a house full of immortals by myself? And they want all of you dead. Yeah, that sounds like the best New Year's ever." Acacia was attempting humor but I could tell she was afraid.

Arabella sat forward and turned her head toward Rowan. "Maybe there's another way. Do we really have to kill her? We could figure out a way for you to switch allegiances without so much risk."

She was back peddling. Acacia was safe for the moment, and she wouldn't put her at risk again. I'd like to think she was also protecting Rowan and myself but she still wouldn't look at me.

"I'm afraid we are way past that, Ara. This isn't about getting me, or even Victor back, it's about making you pay for being born." Rowan pulled the cell out of his pocket and opened the messages. "My contact on the inside tells me that Seraphine's people have the hospital in Montana surrounded, as well as a hotel in northern Idaho, and the River's residents is also covered. If we do not settle this tomorrow, both your families' lives will be over."

I stood and paced the room. There had to be another way. If Arabella was so damned important, why would Rowan be putting her at so much risk? I was clearly missing something. Plus, what part of the plan was he leaving out? He told me 'our reactions needed to be genuine' but what did that mean? I knew I could pull it off but Arabella was probably the worst liar I'd ever met.

"What if I begged Seraphine's forgiveness? You know the house better than anyone and could get Arabella safely through," I said.

Rowan shook his head. "Seraphine hasn't trusted you since you left for Montana, mate. She sent me to check on you, remember? I'm sure if she could have, she would have revoked your agreement a hundred times over."

"Revoked your agreement?" Arabella asked. "What does that mean?"

Acacia let out a breath. "It's one of the lesser known ways to kill an immortal. The living immortal can take back the gift of immortality."

Arabella finally caught my eye. The horror and understanding of Acacia's words sinking in. She could end my life if she wanted. That kind of power over another person is a lot to bear, especially since I was one of her least favorite people on the planet.

She looked back at her hands and tapped her foot in thought. "I think we need to stick with Rowan's plan, but I need some reassurances first."

"Name them," Rowan said.

"If everything goes bad and I can't get out, I want you all to swear yourselves back to Seraphine. You too, Acacia."

"No way!" Acacia yelled.

"This isn't negotiable. If you can't get out, then you're all in. All of you." Arabella shook her head. "If we stick to the plan, we can do this."

The doorbell rang and she locked eyes with me again. She would do this or die trying. No one would be left behind, except for her. If anyone understood that, it was me.

* * *

I listened to the rest of the plan and both Acacia's and Arabella's questions but didn't participate. Once the wine was delivered, I attempted to numb my feelings. The thought of Rowan taking Arabella's blood was beyond anything I was comfortable with. The decision was made without me and I had no choice but to concede. If we survived this, I planned on beating the shit out of him but I couldn't come up with a better way to incapacitate Seraphine.

I excused myself to my room well before sunrise. The girls were watching an old action movie on Joseph's tablet. The house didn't appear to have a TV. Rowan had snuck out at some point but my ability to care was gone. If I thought I could have gotten the girls out and on the road before he returned, I would have done it.

Luck was not on my side since he was back before I even repacked my own bag. Instead, I downed an entire third bottle of wine and attempted to think of anything besides tomorrow.

Something woke me much later. I rolled to the middle of the bed and was surprised to find I was not alone. My breath caught in my throat and I made myself still.

Arabella stood beside my bed with her arms wrapped around her body as if she was holding herself together. Fragile wasn't a word I'd use lightly when describing her but right now it was the only thing that came to mind. I wanted nothing more than to wrap her in my arms and promise everything was going to be okay, but I wasn't what she needed. Besides, I wouldn't make a promise I couldn't keep.

"It's done," she whispered.

My eyes closed and I swallowed my disappointment. The plan was in motion. Rowan had taken her blood. We had only hours until the final confrontation. But why was she here? I was clearly upset about the plan but she didn't owe me anything.

When she sat on the side of the bed facing away from me, I too pulled myself into a sitting position. Her breathing was slow and steady, shoulders back in resolve. Yet, she kept her back to me.

"If we're going to die tomorrow, you need to know…" Her voice was low.

I waited a few seconds. "Know what?"

Suddenly we were face to face. Her hands on my shoulders, golden eyes glowing faintly. I lost all coherent thought. She bit her lip and looked down. Her hand slowly moved up and behind my neck.

"That I feel the same thing as you when I take your blood."

Her lips were against mine tentative at first but the kiss deepened at my response. I pressed her against me and there was no resistance. Her fingers entwined in mine and I didn't feel the bite of her ring. I tried to tell her everything I felt without words.

"Victor?" Arabella's voice was far away but that didn't make sense when she was so close.

"Victor?" This time her voice was clearer.

I opened my eyes and she was standing next to my bed, arms once again wrapped around herself. Her eyes didn't glow. She stood still for a moment then shook her head and turned to leave. It had all been a dream. And with my luck, it was interrupted by real life.

"Wait," I whispered and she stopped. "Are you okay?"

Her shoulders fell but she kept her back turned. "It's done, with Rowan, I mean. I wanted to ask you something, but it doesn't matter. There's at least another couple of hours before sunset. I'm sorry I woke you."

I sat up and leaned back against the headboard. "Why don't you let me decide if it doesn't matter."

"Rowan said," she paused. "that me having your persuasion might come in handy tonight."

I pushed my hair back. "He's not wrong."

"I won't ever make you do something you don't want," she whispered.

"Arabella, if you know anything about me, you know I don't do anything I don't want."

"He said you'd say that too." Arabella turned back to face me. "Victor, open the window."

I got to my feet and took two steps before my brain caught up. My hand was reaching for the shade, my control was no longer my own. I was going to open the west facing window and I was going to burn.

"Stop! Please, stop." Arabella's voice was shaking as I lowered my hand. "I'm sorry. I had to be sure."

"Is that what you wanted to ask?" my voice was quiet with anger.

I couldn't face her. The control she had over me was more than I could comprehend. She wouldn't need to revoke my life, she could just say the word and I would do it myself. Her hand brushed against my shoulder.

"I agree that having a bit of persuasion would be helpful in case we get held up. But you seem uncomfortable when I take your blood, and I'm having trouble…" She paused as if looking for the right words. "I don't like how I feel when I do either."

I desperately wanted to ask what she meant but now was not the time. "Personally, I think we should take Acacia and just run, but running has never solved anything."

She nodded and once again turned to leave. "I'll see you in a few hours."

"Arabella, we need every advantage we can against Seraphine. My feelings be damned." What I didn't say was: *I'd give you every last drop if it meant keeping you alive.*

Chapter Twenty-Four

After the dream and sharing my blood with Arabella, I needed a long and very cold shower. I'd been purposely avoiding everyone as my emotions were raging in every direction. Everything about this plan felt wrong. Even after what I told Arabella, I still wanted to run.

There was a light knock on my door as I finished packing the last of my belongings. I glanced at my watch. It was almost time to leave.

"Come in."

"Rowan says we're leaving in ten minutes." Acacia sounded timid.

I adjusted the cuffs of my shirt before zipping up my bag and turning. She was dressed in a floor length black wrap dress with red trim. Her hair was pulled to the side in an intricate braid that fell over her shoulder. The black eye makeup and red lipstick enhanced her pale complexion. I could see why my sister was so enamored with her.

"You look very nice, Acacia."

A quick smile peeked through her usual resting bitch face. "You look pretty good yourself. Too bad you're still you."

With that, she turned and left the room. Yep, I liked this little shit. A genuine smile crossed my face and I hefted my bag onto my shoulder. Voices downstairs told me everyone was waiting on me.

When I descended the stairs, the first thing I saw was Rowan's powder blue tux. If I needed another reason to strangle the man, I couldn't find it. Subtlety was part of our plan. There was nothing subtle about that fashion disaster.

Acacia was attempting to tie his bowtie but it kept sticking up on one side. When Arabella gently stepped between them and reached for the it, everything else fell away.

She was wearing what could only be described as a deep red ball gown. Black beads and satin details were added in just the right amount to make the dress a true work of art. The corset bodice was tied in the back with both red and black satin ribbons. Her hair was braided with such intricacy that at first, I thought it couldn't be real. Black rose shaped beads sparkled in the light as did her caramel and saffron highlights. She was wearing her wedding dress on the night that may lead to her death.

After fixing Rowan's tie, Arabella turned her back to me as Acacia spoke. "You need a necklace. You're all boob."

Arabella looked down at her ample cleavage. "It's not like I had time to think about accessories, Acacia. This will just have to do."

My hand went to my right pocket. The necklace there suddenly felt like a lead weight. Now wasn't the time but I may never get another one. Without further hesitation, I put my bag down and quickly crossed the room.

Before she could turn, I looped the chain around her neck and fixed the clasp. Her hand lifted as it gently lay against her chest. She let out a sigh and turned. The wall she'd put up crumbled and she gave me a timid smile. Everything about this moment was fucked up.

“I’d never let you go unprepared.”

When I looked at the necklace, my eyes flicked to the scars where her neck and shoulder met. Her skin was flawless but these remained. Why had those stayed? The answer was like a punch to my gut. They stayed because I gave them to her. My blood would never fix them, a glaring reminder of our history.

I cleared my throat, stepped back, and scanned the room. “Where’s Joseph?”

Acacia was the one who answered. “He left after braiding our hair. He’s kind of a cool weirdo.”

Rowan clapped his hands together. “Truer words have never been spoken. Let’s hit the road.”

Arabella’s dress was not really made for long car rides, but she had already thought of that. The skirt portion came off and she wore a pair of black leggings underneath, as well as a pair of black running shoes. If it wasn’t such a good idea, I would have called the Fashion Police myself. Acacia’s matching shoes were visible when she stepped into the van too. It’s like Arabella did this for a living.

* * *

The long drive was quiet, even the radio seemed to grate on everyone’s nerves. Arabella and Acacia played a game on some scratch paper and talked about nothing to pass the time. They’d opted to sit in the back while Rowan drove.

I was nearly convinced we had this until we took the exit to Seraphine's house. Two black Suburbans took up the spaces in front and behind us. The two-lane road allowed them to box us in.

"Rowan, is this part of the plan?" Arabella asked.

Rowan checked his rearview mirror then gunned the van. The SUV in front veered to the left but Rowan anticipated and passed on the right shoulder. Debris spun up under the vehicle and we fishtailed.

Rowan urged the van forward and for a moment, I thought we'd get ahead of the SUVs. Why weren't they chasing us? I was watching in the side mirror so I missed the truck as it smashed into the Rowan's side of the van.

Everything happened so quickly. Glass and grit exploded inward as we rolled onto the passenger side. Metal screamed as the van continued to slide.

The back of the van was wrenched open before I could figure out which way was up. Light filled the space and I could hear Arabella yelling. Both her and Acacia's voices were getting further away. Rowan was suspended by his seat belt above me. I reached out and shook him.

"Not part of the plan, mate," he groaned.

Hands grabbed me from the back. I latched onto the wrist and snapped it. A man's voice cried out. The sound seemed to bring Rowan's consciousness back. He struggled with his seatbelt as another set of hands grabbed him from behind. Three gunshots rang out and everyone froze.

A commanding voice followed. “Seraphine wants the girl alive. You two were optional. Keep resisting and maybe no one will make it to the big house in one piece.”

Rowan met my eyes and nodded. We were royally fucked. I pushed away whomever was trying to pull me toward the back of the van and moved there myself. Once standing, I put my hands up like an idiot.

Everyone looked a bit disheveled but no one was seriously hurt. Part of Acacia’s braid had come undone and her skirt was ripped. The shoulder of my suit jacket and shirt were shredded where I’d come into contact with the road. Someone had handed Arabella her skirt, which she was currently refusing to put back on.

“We’re going to a party,” Rowan said as he dusted himself off. “Listen to the nice man and get dressed.”

I scrutinized his words and noticed he didn’t use her name. The voice had said they needed “the girl” alive but these imbeciles didn’t know which one. We still had a slight advantage.

We were herded separately into the black SUVs. Rowan and Arabella in one, Acacia and I in the other. Being separated was torture, even though I could see the other vehicle ahead of us as we made our way down the long private drive.

“Victor, what are we going to do?” Acacia hissed at me.

“Shut up back there,” one of Seraphine’s goons snapped.

I took Acacia's hand in mine and gave it a squeeze of encouragement. When I loosened the grip, she didn't let go. We were silent the rest of the short trip.

Cars lined the drive when we approached but there was just enough room for the two SUVs right up front. The house was lit up and I knew the party was in full swing. Arabella and Rowan were removed from the car ahead of us and were halfway up the stairs before we followed.

Arabella looked back at Acacia but the goon manhandling her turned her sharply and told her to keep going. The look she gave him was downright murderous. I tensed in case she snapped so I could follow her lead.

"Finally!" Seraphine called from the main door. "I thought you would never get here in time for the midnight countdown. Hurry up. We're all waiting."

Her silver ball gown was dripping with crystals and her blue eyes danced with madness. We'd walked right into her plan.

* * *

While I expected to be escorted past the party to a more private area of the house, Seraphine motioned for us to be brought to the center of it all. The main room had been emptied save for a white grand piano and long tables against one wall.

I didn't recognize the woman playing the piano. The tune was something modern but played in a Classical style. She pointedly ignored us as if her life depended on the music being perfect. With Seraphine, it probably did.

Seraphine picked up a champagne flute from the far table and tapped it gently to get everyone's attention.

"Without order there is chaos. This is the creed we live by." She took a sip of champagne and walked slowly to where we had been left in the middle of the room. "Victor, you invited chaos in when you brought that *thing* into my home."

I struggled against the goon holding my arms. He was beyond strong, meaning he was an old immortal who had recently fed. Not that I'd get far if I had escaped his grasp, we were surrounded by more than five dozen immortals beholden to Seraphine. Our only chance had been the element of surprise.

Seraphine slowly circled us, taking in every detail. "Rowan?"

"Yes, my liege?" he replied and lowered his gaze.

Seraphine faced him then motioned for his release. "Thank you for being such a loyal clan member for so long. Your poor decision has been forgiven as you have brought the real traitors back to me for judgment."

"You son of a bitch!" I yelled and struggled again.

Seraphine walked up and slapped me across the face. "Language! There are ladies present."

"Hey!" Arabella yelled, making Seraphine jump. "Your problem is with me, right? How about you stop dancing around the issue and let's get down to it?"

Seraphine regarded her for a moment then moved to stand in front of Acacia. They were nearly the same height with Seraphine's heels. Seraphine reached up and tugged on a piece of hair that had fallen from her braid then made a tsk noise.

"You know, we don't turn first borns because they are so unpredictable. However, you look about as dangerous as a wet paper bag. How disappointing."

Acacia spit in Seraphine's face. The living immortal closed her eyes and stood still for several seconds before lifting her hand to wipe her cheek. Her eyes screamed murder but she smiled brightly.

She patted Acacia's cheek. "You look a little pale, my dear. How about a bit of sun?"

The goon picked up Acacia and started to walk away. She bucked and fought but was no match for the vampire more than twice her size. Arabella started screaming for Seraphine to listen to her. I looked at Rowan; that two-faced bastard just watched them go. They were taking her to the sunroom. We only had a few hours before she burned. Goddammit! If this wasn't part of the plan, we were all going to die.

"Rowan, you prick! How can you just stand there? I thought we were friends. Help her!" I yelled.

Rowan adjusted his stance and watched Acacia disappear around the corner. His face was a stone wall. I'd never seen him so detached but it appeared I still knew nothing about him.

Seraphine finally faced Arabella. "You could have made a great toy for me. I know Victor would have enjoyed playing with you some more. Isn't that right?"

My blood ran cold. This wasn't going to be a quick death. She was going to isolate Arabella from everything she had and break her before she finally gave her the sweet release of death. I needed to get free so I could take Arabella and Acacia far away from here.

"Seraphine, listen to me." I poured every drop of persuasion into my words. "I helped bring her back to you, even convinced her to change her sister so you could have a new pet. I didn't know what she was when I brought her here but I know now that she can't be allowed to live."

Arabella's head swung in my direction, her eyes wide with shock. She believed me. Deep down, she still thought I hated her for the interrupted binding. That all I ever wanted was her death.

"Oh, my sweet Victor." Seraphine attempted to take another drink of champagne but the glass was empty. Someone rushed forward with a replacement. "You had so much potential but you chose love over power. Never in a million years would I have guessed that you would be so stupid. Now I just have to decide which is more painful. Having her watch as her entire family dies, including you, or having you watch as she dies."

A small blonde woman with huge glasses scurried forward with a tablet. I'd met her before but never cared enough to learn her name. She whispered something to Seraphine and pointed at the screen.

"It appears your arrival was not a minute too soon. The countdown to the new year is about to begin. Everyone grab a glass and get ready to toast to another year!"

Many in the group hesitated but once a few people started getting flutes, the rest quickly followed. We were the main event; the lesson for the new year. Their living immortal was reminding them what breaking the rules looked like.

Seraphine handed her glass to the blonde woman and clapped her hands. One of her regular bodyguards appeared with a sword. I knew nothing about swords but this looked old, heavy, and wicked sharp. Another man followed with a padded chair.

Arabella was forced to her knees with her chest pressed against the chair. Seraphine was going to remove her head at midnight and there was nothing I could do to stop it! Rowan still hadn't moved but his expression had changed from stony to angry. When would he stop this? Please let this be the plan he wouldn't share with me. I couldn't let Arabella die. She was everything.

A bell sounded from hidden speakers above to signal the countdown. Everyone started at ten and slowly counted down. Seraphine hefted the sword and grinned like a mad woman. Arabella thrashed against her restraints as tears of frustration splashed on the marble floor.

Chapter Twenty-Five

"Four!"

"Three!"

"Two!"

"That will be enough, Seraphine!" a voice bellowed from the main entrance.

Everyone froze when tiny pieces of silver tinsel started falling from the ceiling as the clock struck midnight. Seraphine looked toward the door and shrieked in frustration. She attempted to lower the heavy sword but a man stepped from the crowd, catching her arm mid-arc. Recognition dawned when I focused on Joseph's calm demeanor. How had I not seen him?

He gently extracted the sword from her grip but she continued to shout in French at him and then at the man who had stopped her. She backed up and the crowd followed suit, forming a semicircle around her as she continued to scream profanities.

"I said, that is *enough*!" the voice sounded again, slightly closer.

Joseph helped Arabella so she was sitting on the chair then stood between her and Seraphine. The sword down at his side looked a little too natural. I had to tear my eyes away from the two of them because while I still didn't believe she was safe, I needed to know who held such sway over Seraphine.

The crowd near the door parted and a man stepped forward. I blinked and looked again. It was the man from the painting, the one with no name plate. He looked like he had literally stepped from the portrait itself. His military dress was centuries old in design but clearly brand new. The medals on his chest glinted in the light.

"No! No! No!" Seraphine's voice was frantic. "You aren't supposed to be here."

The man stopped about ten feet from her and sighed. "You invite me to your New Year's party every year. This tradition never held much interest for me but this year your other curriculars required my attention."

Without turning, he spoke with unquestionable authority. "Please release this man and retrieve the little one from the sunroom."

Rowan walked over to the goon holding me and sucker punched him. He let go and stumbled backward. Without a word to me, my friend turned heel and walked quickly toward the back of the house to collect Acacia. He and I would have some serious words about this once I figured out what the hell was going on.

"You can't order my people around," Seraphine snapped.

She lunged for the sword held by Joseph but he turned and caught her by the back of the dress, holding her from the floor. She thrashed like a pissed off kitten.

The man walked over to Arabella and helped her to her feet. "It's so nice to see you again, Lovely Arabella."

"Have we met?" Arabella narrowed her eyes at him.

He nodded. "Time doesn't hold the same meaning for me but to you it was a very long time ago. The Council follows all of the potential living immortals from birth. Let me reintroduce myself. I am Pierre Chatelain, leader of the Immortal Council."

He paused as if this should mean something to her but she just continued to stare at him. "I'm sorry but this is all very new to me. I didn't even know I was a living immortal until a few days ago."

"That will not do," he said, then looked around at the crowd.

No one seemed to know what was going on. Seraphine continued to fight against Joseph's grip. I desperately wanted to go to Arabella but I didn't want this Pierre's scrutiny just yet.

"Have you taught your clan nothing of the Council?" He spoke to Seraphine who just hissed at him, which made him clench his gloved hands. The motion made her stop struggling for a moment as if that motion held deep memories.

"You do not rule here. This is my clan. This is my land!" Seraphine spat. "You are outnumbered. My clan is loyal and will destroy you."

Pierre walked forward and back handed her across the face. Blood and saliva sprayed from her mouth and dripped onto her crystal gown. Her look of outrage darkened further but she didn't speak again.

"You will not talk to your Council leader that way and you will most certainly not speak to your father with such insolence."

He nodded and Joseph carried Seraphine from the room. She was still hurling insults in both English and French as they disappeared. Her clan began to murmur in confusion. Yet, no one dared move from their spots.

Pierre lifted his hands to silence the crowd. "I regretfully take full responsibility for my daughter's actions. She will always be my sweet girl and I therefore tend to overlook her transgressions. We shall both be punished for our sins against the Council."

No one moved or spoke so he continued, "Reborn immortals must be supported by a clan. Rogues are not tolerated and will be put to death as per Council law. Seraphine will not be allowed to rule a clan for some time yet to be determined. You can come with me now or," he turned back to where Arabella was standing, "you can follow her."

Arabella took a step back and let out a small laugh. "Oh no. That's not…"

"Come now. This is your birthright. You have already created one reborn. Many more will follow. This world is not something a living immortal can navigate themselves. You will need help. Do not turn it away."

"I don't want this responsibility. I don't want to make more reborn. I just want to go back to my old life."

Pierre took her hands in his. "That is precisely why you are perfect for the job. You have spent your entire life protecting others and you genuinely care. This trait has been lost by so many over the centuries."

He looked around the room again and raised his voice. "Everyone who wishes to join my clan, follow Joseph. He will provide details on travel."

"But I can't take care of anyone else. I can barely afford to take care of myself and," Arabella swallowed hard and lowered her voice, "I don't even have a place to live."

The room had emptied except for two others when Rowan and Acacia returned. The sisters embraced. Pierre watched with a satisfied smile.

"I told you the Council follows all living immortals from birth." He snapped his fingers and a very thin man with an impressive mustache hurried forward with a thick folder. "Arabella, you are a Goddess among vampires and humans alike. You will be treated as such, within the boundaries of the Council. Something my daughter seems to have forgotten, but I digress. Your new home is nearly complete. We had to rush a few things due to your untimely death."

This was the first time Pierre turned his eyes in my direction and I felt the power there. He did not like me and he was clearly not someone I wanted as an enemy.

He broke eye contact and turned to Rowan who got down on one knee and lowered his head. "You have trodden a very thin line and I do believe this time you have crossed it. Punishment must be dealt. You have betrayed two living immortals to which you were bound. To make sure you do not repeat this infraction, I am sentencing you to three centuries as Steward to Arabella. If you even consider another coup, you will be put to death. Do you understand?"

Rowan nodded but did not rise. Pierre turned back to Arabella. "There are five reborn still here.

Are there any you wish to banish from your clan? Think carefully because I will only make this offer once."

Arabella turned to see the blonde woman with the tablet and a bald guy who looked like a gladiator standing near the back of the room. Lastly, she met my eyes. If my heart could have stopped, it would have. She was going to banish me!

She broke eye contact and focused on Pierre. "They will all be my clan."

"Then they now owe their lives to you. Please send my regards to your father." With that, he purposely strode from the room.

* * *

Arabella wrapped her arms around her sister again. Acacia broke down into tears as the gravity of the situation fully hit her, reminding me of her youth. The thin man handed the folder to the blonde woman and quickly moved to follow Pierre. Rowan smartly stayed on the other side of the room.

"Mr. River, if you would follow me please," the thin man instructed.

He looked like something out of a Sherlock Holmes novel. His brown suit was highly tailored and his mustache was truly something of note. Blond hair was parted down the middle and meticulously combed down to his ears.

"I think I'll stay." I turned from the man.

"Mr. River? It's not a request."

Arabella noticed our conversation and moved to join us. "I told Pierre that everyone who stayed was part of my clan. Why are you taking him?"

"Pardon, Ms. Arabella, please allow me to introduce myself. I am Mr. Chatelain's personal assistant, François De la Cour. Victor's punishment must be passed down by the entire Council. Mr. Chatelain is not fond of waiting so if we could please proceed."

"Punishment for what?" she demanded.

The thin man frowned. "He is to answer for denying the world a future living immortal."

She sucked in a breath and put her hand to her stomach. His words made no sense to me but they seemed to have a deep meaning to Arabella. She looked at me and tears pricked her eyes then she cleared her throat and spoke to François.

"Victor was not the one who shot me. He didn't even know I was pregnant."

The room tilted and my ears began to ring and I almost missed the thin man's response. "His hand may not have pulled the trigger but his actions led to the death, and yours. Judgment is not mine to give but the Council will need answers. Victor, if you please."

"He's not going with you." Arabella was standing her ground but Rowan grabbed her arm and whispered in her ear. All the fight drained from her and she nodded to François.

I turned and followed him automatically, not trusting myself to make eye contact with her. My brain was numb with this new information. Why had she accepted me into her clan when her hate was so deeply seeded? Had the child been mine? Is that why no one told me?

François led me to a silver limo and began speaking to someone in rapid, angry French. The back seat was empty except for Joseph. As soon as the door closed, the car started moving.

"How are you involved in all this?" I asked him.

"I am Steward to Pierre. Worry not, Victor, no harm will come to your living immortal. She is under the Council's protection until she can provide her own," Joseph explained.

As we drove, the ants under my skin feeling grew. "Where exactly are we going?"

Joseph smiled. "You're in luck. The council members are currently meeting in Salt Lake City so we do not have to travel far to meet with them."

The rest of the drive and the flight were quiet. I was on a plane with a little over a dozen of Seraphine's clan and Joseph. Everyone seemed to be in shock and Joseph refused to talk. Being alone in my head was not safe and I would have killed for a phone. I needed answers.

Once back on the ground, we were loaded into several vans and driven through downtown. I'd heard of the Salt Lake Temple but I'd never seen it in person. A tall white stone fence surrounded the structure. Lights illuminated the internal walls making the spires almost glow. Trees inside and out were covered in colored lights from the holidays. The vans turned and pulled into an underground parking structure under the temple.

Joseph and several others put the travelers into small groups and started leading them into the building. I was part of the last group led by Joseph and I moved closer to him as we started our trek into the basement. Keypads were stationed outside several doors and in all the elevators. The passcodes varied but there was no attempt to hide them.

The basement had cement walls and bare bulbs hung from the ceiling. It felt like we walked for hours either around in circles or down more flights of stairs. The passcodes would be useless, even if someone did decide to leave. Not that anyone would try. It was well known that rogue immortals were immediately put to death. The harm to the entire community was too high a risk for second chances.

I was hopelessly lost by the time Joseph motioned for me to enter a small room. The inside looked like a small hotel room with an attached bath. The door, however, looked like a prison cell made of thick iron bars. There was no doubt that I was being held for a crime. For how long was anyone's guess.

The room had a bed, an armchair, and a small dresser. On the dresser was a Travel Utah magazine and a Book of Mormon. I shook my head. Was this some sort of sick joke? I opened the dresser to find a random assortment of black and gray clothing. The bathroom had a shower stall, sink and toilet. A cabinet held basic toiletries. Even though I had come with nothing, the Council made sure I had the basics.

Sunrise was approaching. I could feel the drain even several stories below ground. I sent a prayer to whatever deity might be listening that Joseph's words were true and Arabella was safe. I'd survive whatever punishment was handed down to me then I'd spend the rest of my immortal life making up for all the terrible things I'd done to her.

Chapter Twenty-Six

Two weeks had painfully dragged by since my arrival in Salt Lake. I'd been outside only once and was allowed to walk the grounds inside the stone walls. Four men I assumed were guards followed at a respectable distance. While several people had passed my room, no one had given me any indication as to what had happened to Seraphine or when I would meet with the Immortal Council.

My hunger gnawed at me. Rowan was right about it taking over every waking thought if too much time had elapsed between meals. I'd memorized the travel magazine and even made an attempt at the Book of Mormon out of sheer boredom. However, I never made it more than ten pages before my mind wandered.

Where was Arabella now? Had Tom recovered? Did they reschedule the wedding? Would Eve ever forgive me for getting her involved in all this? And more importantly and most often, had the child I killed been mine?

Joseph appeared without warning one night and opened my door. He didn't say anything, just stood and waited. I'd been rereading the Utah National Park review for the millionth time in nothing but a pair of sweatpants. When it was clear he wanted me to follow, I grabbed a long-sleeved shirt from the drawer and stuffed my feet into my shoes. They were far too dressy for the rest of my outfit but no other shoes had been offered.

I followed Joseph through the maze of tunnels and elevators again. This time trying to remember the route but was surprised when he opened a door that I was sure would be a stairwell that instead opened to the street outside. A blast of frigid air swirled around us as we exited the building.

We walked in silence as cars and light rail passed by. The downtown area was clean and bright even in the late evening. People hurried past in the cold January wind. I could hear blood rushing through their veins when they drew near. Another day or two and I wouldn't be safe.

Joseph stopped in front of what appeared to be a bar and grill. There was a sign on the door reading "This is a restaurant, not a bar." I looked questioningly at Joseph who just shrugged.

Thankfully, the hostess seated us near the fireplace in the back as I was barely in control. She left both food and drink menus then promised our server would be by shortly. The light was soft and music almost too quiet. I glanced around the room in search of…

Joseph's voice cut through my blood haze. "The Council wishes to apologize for the delay. Other matters have been more pressing and they are having trouble finding documentation on how to deal with your specific infraction."

I opened my mouth to ask what he meant when a twenty-something male with a severe undercut and thick red glasses approached the table.

"Hi. I'm Marty. I'll be your server tonight. Can I get some crab dip or jalapeno poppers started for the table?"

Joseph looked at the menu for a moment then ordered. "I'll have the Caesar salad and your holiday ale."

"Excellent. And for you, sir?"

"I'll have a bottle of Malbec." I kept my eyes on Joseph confused as to why he ordered food. I could tell my mind wasn't firing on all cylinders but what was going on?

"I'm sorry, sir but I can't sell you alcohol without a food order."

"You can't what?" I snapped.

"You must be from out of town. We are a restaurant, which means we aren't legally allowed to serve alcohol without a food order." When I continued to stare at him like he was from another planet, he continued. "Also, your friend will either have to finish his beer or wait until the wine is gone. We can't have two alcoholic beverages per person at a table."

"The wine isn't for him." My voice was starting to rise and thoughts moved to draining this idiot dry then enjoying my wine in peace when Joseph spoke.

"Please, forgive my friend. You are correct that he is from out of town. He has been traveling and is quite tired. He'll have your best steak, rare, and just bring him one glass at a time."

Marty gave me a sympathetic look before sauntering away. I must be going crazy from lack of blood. What kind of backwards place was this?

"Utah has some intricate liquor laws but there are ways around them. Please accept the Council's apology for the delay. They are covering this meal and will provide you with whatever else you may need."

I leaned in. "What I need, Joseph, is answers. I'm going stir crazy locked in that room. If they aren't going to meet with me soon, just send me home. It's not like I'm going to run from this. I'm a lawyer. I know how this works."

Joseph regarded me silently for long enough that I figured he was done talking. Our server brought our meals and drinks. I had two empty glasses in front of me before he spoke again.

"Seraphine has been more difficult to manage than originally thought. Her crimes have grown increasingly numerous the more we investigate. Pierre is ready to disown her and is too being punished for not keeping a tighter rein on his daughter."

"That's all well and good but I couldn't give two shits about that little brat. I was brought here to meet with the Council. Is that going to happen or not?"

Joseph nodded. "You will meet with three of the seven council members tomorrow an hour after sunset. A new suit will be brought to you beforehand. Is there anything else you require for this meeting?"

"I don't know, is there? I'm going to answer for something I know nothing about. Are they just sentencing me or do I get to defend myself?"

"I am not privy to Council meetings. Stewards are rarely allowed to attend." Joseph hesitated then continued. "But Pierre tends to speak to himself while solving problems. Sometimes, he forgets I am there. He is not on your side, Victor. The loss of a living immortal from his line is not something he will forgive."

I sat back and finally understood the anger I'd seen in the man's eyes on New Year's Eve. I'd killed his grandchild or great, great, whatever grandchild. Power was important to this man and I'm sure continuing his bloodline was part of that dominance.

"How did they know Arabella's baby," the words were actually difficult to say, "was a living immortal?"

Joseph frowned and tapped his thumb on the table as if considering his answer. Marty stopped by to make sure we had everything we needed and to drop off the check. It took everything I had not to tell him to fuck off.

Joseph finally let out a breath. "Male living immortals can sire children even after their death. Female living immortals can only produce children in life. Records show that all first born children of these women are also immortals regardless of gender."

I thought about this for a while. Tom mentioned that Arabella couldn't have children since she was shot. However, the way he worded it could have been his way of trying to tell me she was pregnant before then. I drained my wine and asked the question I needed to know.

"Was it mine?" Joseph gave me a puzzled look so I clarified. "Was Arabella's child mine?"

Understanding crossed his face and he shook his head. "I'm sorry but I do not know. The restaurant is closing soon. Let's go take care of your other needs. It has been a while since my last meal as well."

* * *

We walked farther from the temple where the lights weren't nearly as bright or as frequent. The late hour and biting cold wind meant the streets were virtually empty. I hoped Joseph had a destination in mind or maybe he was leading me to a group like the one at the safe house in Nevada.

Joseph stopped in front of a nondescript brick building with a fluorescent cross illuminating the only doorway. He nodded and pulled the door open without a word to reveal a dingy reception area.

An exhausted looking older woman with graying brown hair lifted her head and a clipboard in a single motion. "The shelter doesn't have much space tonight so you may have to double up."

Joseph took the clipboard from her and smiled, a drop of persuasion tinged his speech. "We do not seek lodging. We've come to offer a few hours of whatever assistance is needed at your facility tonight."

The woman's eyes lit with such gratitude, her entire appearance changed. The smile made her face light up and a giggle escaped her lips. She put the clipboard back on her side of the desk and stood, smoothing the smock over her ample frame.

"I'm Marigold. There aren't a lot of duties this late but we can always use a couple sets of hands. Let me get you to Raul. He'll get you started."

"Thank you, Marigold. My name is Joseph and this is my friend, Victor."

We followed the woman down the hallway past what appeared to be a dark cafeteria, a light shone in the very back in what I assumed was the kitchen. The next area was also dimly lit and lined with bunk beds or cots. Nearly every bed was full, heartbeats ranged from full relaxation to almost panic. Light snores almost covered the occasional sob.

Raul was a huge man of Hispanic descent. He was pushing a mop when we rounded the corner. Despite the manual labor and late hour, he whistled a happy tune as he worked.

"Raul, Joseph and Victor would like to volunteer for a few hours tonight. Can you help them get started?"

Raul smiled and clapped his enormous hands together. "Welcome. I could use a hand finishing the floors in here. Jingtao would probably appreciate some help in the kitchen. We got a large donation of sweet rolls but they all need to be baked before breakfast."

"I've got the kitchen." I told Joseph as Raul opened the janitor's closet for another mop and bucket.

With a nod, I headed back toward the cafeteria. A tiny Chinese woman was hefting a full sheet pan of cinnamon rolls out of the oven. The full pan probably weighed as much as she did. I grabbed another pair of hot pads and rushed over to take the hot pan before she dropped it.

"I'm here to help," I said as I took the pan from her.

She grinned at me, her smile revealing three missing front teeth. "Xie Xie. Xie Xie."

Her eyes caught me off guard, one gold indicating she was a vampire but the other dark brown. For some reason, her blood didn't call to me like other humans. The kitchen had been a good idea since in my current state, Raul's blood had been very tempting. This woman was altogether different and that intrigued me like nothing had in a long time.

I placed the pan on the baker's rack and grabbed an empty. Jingtao opened another package of frozen cinnamon rolls and motioned for me to place the pan on the prep table. She grabbed a giant spatula of butter and prepped the pan then spaced the frozen rolls evenly.

We worked like this for almost three hours without another word, probably because neither of us knew the other's language but it didn't matter. I appreciated the silence. Once the earlier baked rolls were cool enough, we transferred them to trays and she artfully covered them in a cinnamon cream cheese frosting. I washed the pans so we could reuse them.

"Victor?" Joseph's voice sounded as I dried another pan. "It's time to go."

Jingtao gave me another head bob in thanks. She was busy stirring the giant vat of oatmeal she'd started about half an hour ago.

I met Joseph in the hallway and was about to ask what the plan was when Raul joined us. He led us down a quiet passage and out the back door. Two homeless men were huddled in a sheltered corner with a small dog that at one point had probably been white.

"We don't allow pets inside the shelter. Jasper and Willis won't leave little Cupcake alone so I've made them a place out here to get through the cold night. They've helped with your kind's needs before," Raul explained, giving the dog a biscuit and a scratch behind the ears. "Thanks again for your help tonight. You're always welcome."

Joseph and I took just what we needed from the homeless men. Cupcake kept trying to cuddle, which was weird but made sense due to the cold. Joseph gave them some cash from his wallet and instructed them to stay in a motel for the next two nights because of the dropping temperatures. From the touch of persuasion he added to his words, I knew they would happily comply.

The work had actually felt good and kept my mind off my own troubles for a while. I wondered if that had been Joseph's plan all along. Acacia was correct: a cool weirdo indeed, and a friend. One I hadn't realized I needed until now.

My head felt clearer after feeding and the walk back. I did need a few things before my meeting later tonight and gave him a list as we made our way through the now deserted streets. Joseph promised to do his best to get them for me. When we got back to my room, I hesitated.

"Can I ask one more thing?" Joseph nodded so I continued. "What's with the Book of Mormon and why are we in the basement of the temple?"

Joseph graced me with one of his rare smiles then leaned in like he was sharing a conspiratorial secret. "Most modern religions are controlled by the Immortal Council. Each member has their favorite and tries to convert other immortals to their cause. When you come to Italy, they'll give you a copy of the Old Testament."

"Joseph, thank you for everything." I couldn't help but laugh. "But would it be possible to get something else to read?"

Chapter Twenty-Seven

Just after sunset, a young man I had not seen before opened my door. He was dressed in white button-down shirt, thin black tie, and black slacks. In his hands, he held a charcoal garment bag and a paper grocery sack. I laid the clothing on the bed and looked in the sack. Everything I requested was there, except the phone.

I looked up to inquire about its absence when he spoke. “The final item was not approved at this time.”

“Do you know why?” My mood was decidedly foul not knowing what to expect when I met with the Council later.

He shook his head and quickly left the room. Once the door closed, I realized he was a human, and was frightened. Great. I wondered what rumors were buzzing around about the crazy reborn vampire in the cell?

To distract myself, I unzipped the garment bag and was impressed. This was something I would have chosen for myself. The charcoal gray suit and black shirt still smelled new but were pressed and ready to wear. I hung the entire bag on the hook in the bathroom and started unloading the rest of the items.

It was old fashioned but the legal pad and pens gave me a nostalgic feeling from when I first passed the bar and was junior counsel. A stainless-steel stemless wine glass and bottle of red were next. I grimaced at the twist top but realized that I’d requested a bottle of wine but not a corkscrew. A pair of running shoes, today's newspaper, and some reading material rounded out the contents. The book was a well-worn Western paperback. The magazine was titled Ensign and after a quick glance at the article titles, I could tell it was another Mormon publication. Who knew Joseph had a sense of humor?

An hour later, the jokester himself arrived to escort me to the Council. Being dressed with my basic prep materials made me feel more like myself. The two glasses of wine helped too.

We once again made our way through the basement levels in what felt like circles. At the main level, we exited and walked to one of the smaller buildings within the temple grounds. Nerves kept my mouth shut.

The building had a museum quality feel. Paintings depicting Jesus and his miracles lined the walls. Quotes were stenciled between the paintings to tell the story as we moved through the space. Joseph led me to a set of double doors and turned to stand to the right.

"I will be here when the session concludes."

I nodded and pushed the door open. Three faces turned as I entered, none of whom I recognized. There was an Asian woman, a very dark-skinned man, and what looked like a teenager of Hispanic descent. Considering Seraphine looked no more than eleven, I knew age was not easy to determine for living immortals. None of them seemed to command the room like Pierre but they definitely had power in numbers.

The room looked like a small chapel. The three were seated at a long table to the left of a podium. A smaller table was set up in front of the first row of pews. Clearly, that was my destination. As I approached, the trio stood.

"Mr. River, we will start with introductions then begin the inquiry." The first person to speak was the woman. "I am Councilwoman Tsu. These are Councilmen Imbarra and Gutierrez."

"I was told there were seven council members." I tried to keep my voice level but was annoyed they were going to drag this out.

"The remaining members are currently attending to other matters. You will meet with everyone in time. If you have everything you require, we will begin," she explained then motioned for her colleagues and me to sit. "You have been charged with the death of a future living immortal. These meetings will determine your punishment."

But not my guilt.

That was already decided and after weeks of solitude, I had convinced myself they were right. Knowingly or not, I was responsible for the death of an unborn child and the love of my life. Nothing they did to me could be worse than the punishment I was currently battling within myself.

Councilman Imbarra spoke with a faint South African accent. "In your own words, please explain to us the evening of the event."

I stood to address them. "As you know, the evening in question was the last of my mortal life. Memories within the days leading up to and immediately after are blurry. This is part of the rebirth process."

They leaned in and spoke quietly to each other. After a few moments, they turned back to me and seemed to have agreed on a different approach. A tablet sat on the end of the table near Gutierrez for what I assumed was to record the session. Imbarra picked it up and took a moment to find something.

He folded his hands on the table before he spoke. "We have previously reviewed the witness statements for those present that evening. Since your memory is understandably impacted, we will read the summary to you and focus on reasoning and decisions that led to the event."

Hearing my life being read aloud as if I hadn't experienced it was a very odd feeling and one I did not enjoy. The tone was emotionless but I could tell witnesses were biased. The time gap in my memory was torture in itself and having to defend something I didn't remember seemed unfair.

As I listened to the details, I could tell they had spoken to my mother. Of course, she knew of and would cooperate with the Immortal Council. However, some of the details were clearly from someone else. Considering Arabella and Acacia's ignorance about the Council on New Year's, that left only one person. Tom.

Did he know what he was doing when he answered their questions? I was starting to regret my attempt at repairing that relationship. My brother was trying to beat me at my own game and clearly wanted me out of the picture. Permanently.

The first question took me off guard. "Arabella Simon was in a relationship with your brother, is that correct?"

The past tense caught my attention and once again, I longed for a phone. The indifferent façade I'd put into place cracked. I needed to know what was happening in the outside world and to know for sure she was okay.

I pulled myself back to the present and responded. "That is correct."

"Then why was she being bound to you on the night in question?" Tsu asked.

I'd been rolling around the memories I did have for the last two weeks in preparation. What I found was not going to help me. I was a selfish prick. At the time, I had convinced myself that our relationship was real but now I see it was all a sham.

"Arabella's relationship with my brother was on hold." I intentionally kept my answers vague to test the waters. "She had agreed to marry and be bound to me."

Gutierrez spoke for the first time. "Witnesses say your relationship with the living immortal was forced."

I felt my jaw clench. "She made the decision to stay with me."

Querying continued for hours. None of the council members disagreed with my statements, nor did they agree. The questions were all over but they all focused on my mindset. As my temper was tested, I had to focus to keep my persuasion in check.

Just when I thought I would break, Tsu stood. "Thank you for your time and insight on this matter. You will meet with the remaining council members soon."

When she paused, I spoke. "Councilmembers, while I wait, could I have access to the Immortal Council laws? As you know, I was part of Seraphine's clan and therefore misinformed about its presence."

She hesitated and listened to the other members before answering. "This seems an acceptable request. Copies will be brought to you."

I pushed a bit harder. "Electronic files are fine if they are available."

Imbarra's lips twitched before he cleared his throat to speak. "For the time being, we will continue to limit your communications with the outside world. If there are specific questions for specific contacts, please pass them on to Joseph. He is serving as your liaison during these sessions."

When they rose, I followed suit. My time in the courtroom had conditioned the response. They exited through the back of the room through a door I couldn't see. I glanced down at my notepad and realized I had started taking notes but stopped when I wrote "Tom", which was circled until the page ripped. If by some miracle, the Council decided my life was not forfeit, I would hunt him down and make him pay for his words against me.

Chapter Twenty-Eight

Time seemed to pass more slowly each day. The only way I knew time was progressing at all was the daily pressure of the sun and the newspapers left just outside my door.

Another two weeks passed before Joseph took me out of the temple basement again. We ended up at the same restaurant but this time we had a female server who was more than willing to bend the rules after a little flirting. She even added her phone number to the customer copy of the bill. She would have made a fine meal but I wasn't in a place to make those decisions. Actually, I wasn't making any of my own decisions and it was getting tiresome.

The beat-up paperback ended up being from Joseph's personal collection. He told me of his fascination with the American West and even owned a Palomino at Pierre's estate. However, he hadn't been allowed to travel to the US during the height of the Wild West and that genuinely seemed to bother him. The more I learned about this man, the more I liked him.

I met with the first three council members again and they asked all the same questions then I'd meet with another three than a mixture of both. They ranged in visual age, gender, and race. Their only consistency was belief in my guilt. Councilman Young looked like an elderly prophet complete with long white beard while Patel looked like a Bollywood princess. I kept expecting

Councilman Escobar to pull a sword and make a Z for Zorro. He was by far the most animated of the group.

Chatelain never made an appearance and when I questioned it, I was reminded he too was part of an ongoing investigation. It felt like a stall technique. I was punishing myself mentally as I spent my time locked in my room and maybe that was part of their plan all along.

The same man who dropped off my first care package arrived with several banker boxes early one evening. Since then, I had been immersing myself into the Immortal Council laws. It would take a normal human a lifetime to learn all of these. Good thing I had all the time in the world, at least in theory.

Some of the more antiquated laws and restrictions were downright laughable, others made me wonder what infraction had been committed to require specific amendments be written down. There were restrictions on the minimum age in which a contract could be created between a living immortal and vampire seeking rebirth. Another explained the financial obligations between reborn and living immortal that was entirely one sided, and not in the favor of the reborn. My favorite was the statute explaining the limit on how many bats a living immortal could own.

What I was really searching for were the laws that would ultimately define my punishment. There was very little on their stance on the death of other immortals. Again, they seemed to regard reborn as replaceable and I guess, we were. Only one passage mentioned the death of living immortals.

I read and re-read the passage multiple times trying to find a loophole. I scanned the adjacent regulations but nothing was relevant. The short version was purposely causing the death of a living immortal was punishable by permanent death. There were no exceptions, there were no excuses. Seraphine was so fucked. The only hope I held was the fact that I hadn't known the child existed.

I closed the binder and poured another glass of wine. Joseph had been very helpful in keeping my stash well stocked. The screw top wine had even started to grow on me. Not that I'd need it very much longer. I was scheduled to meet with the full council tomorrow.

As a distraction and break from legal jargon, I opened today's paper. Yet another thing Joseph was more than happy to make sure was delivered daily. I'd learned quite a bit about the area, even though I'd only seen inside the temple grounds and the few blocks to and from the restaurant that Joseph favored. The national section told me nothing had changed overall but it didn't give me the information I needed to know for my sanity.

After browsing the local headlines, I pulled the entertainment section to set aside as I never cared about celebrities and their lives unless I was defending them as clients. As I flipped it over, a photo caught my eye. Slowly, I turned it right side up, not fully understanding what I was seeing.

The photo was of my brother with a young boy at a park. That in and of itself was not what gave me pause. It was the fact the little boy looked just like we had at that age but with curly hair. There was a woman slightly out of focus behind them. As I squinted, I thought it might be Arabella with short hair. The article continued further in and I tore the sheet turning the pages. *Love Child for Everyone's Favorite New Alt Rock Star?* was the article's headline.

The picture on the second page showed Tom holding the boy's hand and his arm was around the woman's shoulder. Rachel. She smiled up at him like he was the sun. I'd seen that smile too many times but never directed at me. I read the article looking for more information but it all seemed like conjecture.

I sat back and tried to wrap my head around this new information. While I still had no idea if Arabella's baby was mine or Tom's, there was no doubt that the boy in the photos was his. Rachel and I hadn't been together for almost a year before the night I almost drained her dry. Had Tom known about this kid the whole time?

No, there was no way he had known. Tom wanted a family as much or more than he wanted to be famous. The fact that he was possibly dying in the hospital must have brought Rachel out of the woodwork. When we had been fighting over her, my life was completely wrapped up in winning her affections. Now, I looked at the two of them together and felt absolutely nothing.

That wasn't entirely true. My first thought was whether Arabella knew, and if she did, how she was coping? Her entire life seemed to have been ripped away in a matter of months. Considering both their lengthy engagement and her reaction to his harsh words about immortality made me wonder if she had been having second thoughts about the two of them long before I showed back up. Hope flared in me but I squashed it. There was a good chance I would never see her again.

I walked to my door and peered down the hall. It was empty. My hand slammed against the bars in frustration. I'd gotten used to not communicating with anyone but enough was enough. I slammed the bars again and started yelling.

During the walks to and from my room, I'd noticed cameras installed at strategic locations. I knew there was one about twenty feet to the left of my room. I waved in the direction and continued to yell for a few minutes. There was no movement or sound to indicate anyone was paying any attention to my tantrum and I began to feel like a fool.

I needed to focus on tomorrow. Only a miracle could get me out of this place. My head needed to be in the game, not on happenings I had no control over. Tom had inadvertently given me something more to fight for. Until today, I was sure Arabella was happily married by now and probably glad that I was otherwise occupied. Hope was a dangerous thing but it was all I had.

I was re-reading a passage from the last box of binders when I heard my door open. Joseph stood in the doorway looking uncomfortable, which was very uncharacteristic.

"I had a moment of weakness but I need to prepare for tomorrow," I said, looking away from him. He was silent long enough that I finally turned back. "What do you want?"

"I've been in communication with Arabella's Steward. He wishes to speak with you before the final council meeting." He held a phone in my direction but did not move from blocking the doorway.

As he transferred the cell phone to my hand, I hated how much I felt dependent on something so small. Joseph was going out on a limb by bringing this to me. My constant request for either a phone or laptop had been denied every time. I didn't want to speak to Rowan but there were questions I had to know before my judgment.

A phone number was queued up and I pressed the call button. One, two, three rings then a pause.

"Give me a minute." Rowan's voice was muffled and I heard female voices in the background. "How's my best mate?"

So many responses crossed my mind so I went with the clearest message. "You're a fucking asshole."

Rowan's laughter grated on my nerves and I almost hung up but there must be a reason he was reaching out now. "I miss you too. But remember I told you, I needed you to follow my lead and everything went according to plan. When have I ever steered you wrong?"

"I don't believe you for one second." I rubbed my temple and tried to calm down. "You needed to talk to me about something?"

There was a short pause. "Arabella's alright, mate. It's been a little hit and miss but she's okay."

I had so many questions but he knew what I needed to hear the most and, in that moment, I began to forgive him. "Thank you, but somehow, I don't think that is why you insisted on sneaking a phone call to me."

Joseph still stood in the doorway. His expression told me that I wasn't supposed to be getting this call. Somehow, he had decided to help me, even if he was punished in return.

"You got me there, bruv. I've been pouring over the Council laws trying to find something in your favor." He paused. "Statute 180.4.1, look it up. Memorize it. It's your only chance. I'm not ready to do this on my own. Whether or not Arabella realizes it yet, she needs you too."

I scribbled the numbers on the corner of the newspaper. Joseph hurried in and swiped the phone from me then dropped it into his pocket in one fluid motion. In his other hand was another western paperback.

"Since you finished the first one, I thought you'd like the second in the series."

As I took the book from his hand, I glanced up to see Imbarra walking past as if it was part of his normal routine. His gait was slow and he never turned his head in my direction but it was clear he was checking up on me. None of the council members had walked through the basement the entire time I'd been here. Someone besides Joseph saw my outburst and decided I was up to something.

"Thank you." I handed him the entertainment section of the paper. "There were some interesting headlines today. Maybe you could look into this one for me?"

I tapped on the picture of Tom and his eyes widened. Clearly, he had not looked at the paper before dropping it off or I probably wouldn't have seen the article at all. I had no idea how much of my past he knew but somehow, I was pretty sure it was more than I knew about him. He gently folded the paper under his arm and nodded.

Once he was gone, I started looking for whatever Rowan thought was going to save me. The binders were labeled by section: 79, 132, 197, 14. In my frantic research, I'd started putting the binders back into the boxes at random. This was going to take some time.

An hour later, I had everything in order and back into the boxes. The binder that held the laws in the 180s section was not here. Considering Rowan's claim that it was my only hope, I doubted it was an oversight.

I sat back on my heels and stared at the bars on my door. How was I going to use it in my favor if I had no idea what it was?

* * *

I felt unprepared when I woke at sunset. Try as I might, the pull of sleep was still too strong. Joseph assured me as time went on, I'd be able to set my own sleep schedule but as a newborn, didn't love that comparison, my body was still in transition. When I asked how long, he just shrugged.

My legal pad was nearly full of notes at this point. It held all the questions that had been asked, quirks I'd noticed about each council member, and things that were going to damn me. I wish I could say the last part was a short list but the further the Council dug into my mortal life, the more I realized how shitty of a person I really had been.

Joseph appeared two hours later. His face was stoic as he opened the door and took a step inside. This was odd since we were leaving, until he reached out. A patch of white was in his palm and he carefully transferred it to me as if giving me a final handshake before the gallows.

"I was unable to find any more information about the newspaper article," he said a little too loudly.

I unrolled the paper and quickly read the neat script. He had found the statute Rowan asked for! Once the words permeated my brain, Joseph nodded and motioned toward the door.

I hurried back to my makeshift desk. "Can you get this to Arabella, please?"

He hesitated then took the sheets of folded paper. I had no envelope so there was no way to know if he would read the contents before it was mailed. It didn't matter because I had convinced myself I was never going to see her again, even if by some miracle I lived out the rest of this day.

Our destination turned out to be a different building than our other meetings. This one was much bigger, more like an auditorium than a chapel. There was a stage and behind it rows and rows of elevated seating. My mind went back to a Christmas program we'd watched as a family years ago with the Mormon Tabernacle choir. The TV hadn't given the space the justice it deserved.

The Immortal Council was seated on the stage. Instead of the dress clothes they had been wearing during all our other meetings, this time they all wore black robes. It felt less like a panel of judges and more like seven executioners. Their conversations died as I approached.

While the leader of the Immortal Council had been absent at all the previous meetings and my inquiry as to his whereabouts deflected, that was not the case today. He wouldn't have missed this for the world.

Pierre Chatelain's smile was as cold as they come. The meetings and questions were a waste of time. He had made his decision long before my arrival and as leader, his would be the final vote.

"Have a seat, Mr. River." He motioned to the single chair placed before the stage.

I observed each of the council members as I made my way toward them. Several nodded or smiled in a sad way when they made eye contact, others continued to chat amongst themselves. Once I was standing next to the chair, the entire group turned to stare me down.

"You are here to answer for the murder of a future living immortal. Thank you for taking the time to answer all our questions. Your perspective went a long way in determining the appropriate sentence. Shall we begin?" Chatelain asked.

"I would like to remind the Immortal Council of statute 180.4.1." My voice carried louder than I intended but the sound quality of this room was amazing, making me sound much more confident than I currently felt.

Councilwoman Tsu hurried to the laptop in front of Gutierrez and started typing. She scanned the screen twice then stood upright and looked at Chatelain.

"180.4.1 states: A council member cannot pass sentence on an infraction related to his or her direct family line," she recited.

Chatelain's face darkened and he rushed to the laptop and read the passage under his breath. He looked up at me and there was murder in his eyes. Not only would he not be passing judgment on me, but he also wouldn't be able to pass a lenient sentence for his daughter either.

"How is it you know Council law better than its leaders?" Patel asked.

I scanned the group then focused on Chatelain. "I requested copies of Immortal Council's laws shortly after my arrival. I took it upon myself to study them as I planned on requesting to be legal counsel for my clan once released."

"You did not receive a copy of this one!" Chatelain exclaimed, realized his mistake, then forged on a breath later. "The statute matters not.

The Council has voted and your sentence is the end of your immortal life."

You could have heard a pin drop and all eyes were on Chatelain. Some faces were turned in adoration, others with pity. He was losing his control, first because of the infractions of his daughter and now because of me. I'd just solidified him as a very dangerous enemy.

Councilwoman Tsu moved to stand next to Chatelain, placing a hand on his arm. "Mr. River, if you would please exit the same way you arrived? We will need a moment to deliberate amongst ourselves. Your liaison should still be waiting."

Chatelain turned sharply and looked at her in disbelief. Keeping my stride steady, I made the climb back up to the double doors. It took everything I had not to run to them.

Joseph looked genuinely surprised when I exited the room. "It's over?"

"No. Rowan's last second Hail Mary may have just saved my life."

I took two deep breaths and let them out slowly to ground myself. My ears strained to hear anything inside but the room was clearly soundproof. I focused on nothing else for at least twenty minutes then gave up.

Joseph watched me with a concerned look. He opened his mouth twice but did not speak. Without a word, he took up his previous position in front of the door.

"What aren't you saying?" I demanded.

His shoulders dropped and he turned his head back to me. "I consider you a friend, Victor, and I don't have many. I watched your interactions with the living immortal at the safe house and read the letter you wished to send her. There are worse things than death."

"What does that mean?"

The door opened and Gutierrez motioned me back inside. I tried to catch Joseph's eye again but he had turned his back once more. There was no choice but to follow the councilman and accept my sentence.

Chapter Twenty-Nine

Only six council members remained on the stage. Chatelain was noticeably missing and Tsu had taken his place in the center. There was a feeling of division in the room.

Tsu waited until Gutierrez was seated in front of the laptop and nodded he was ready. As with every other meeting I'd had with the Council, he was responsible for recording the proceedings. In another world, I think I would have liked him.

"Let the record state Councilpersons Imbarra, Gutierrez, Patel, Escobar, and Young are in attendance and acting Leader Councilwoman Tsu will be passing down the sentence to Victor River for denying the world a future living immortal."

The fact that her description was different from Chatelain's made me wonder if her stance was also in my favor. I set my notebook on the chair. This was not going to take long.

"Your actions against the living immortal Arabella Simon led to the death of something we hold more dear than anything else on this planet. Living immortals are very rare. Having two born within a century is a gift we have only received a precious few times before. You have shared your recitation of these events and we have reviewed witness statements from the time in which your memory has been altered." Tsu paused for Gutierrez to catch up. "The Council has voted on your sentence. Do you have anything to add before it is passed upon you?"

Closing arguments. Why was I so unprepared? They had picked apart my entire time with Arabella. Exposed things buried so deep in my memory that I could never pull them back to the surface. Nothing I could say now would matter.

"I have nothing further."

"Very well. Victor Lucian River, your sentence is three-fold. First, you can be called upon at any time to assist in Council infraction reviews for current and future immortals as an impartial third party effective immediately. You will not be able to refuse these summonses unless you are currently defending one of your own clan members. Second, you will not be allowed to contact your clan or clan leader during this or future sessions." She paused and looked at the rest of the Council as if to make sure they were all in agreement with the final portion. "Lastly, you took away our greatest hope. Now, we will take away yours. During your immortality, you are forbidden from pursuing or accepting a relationship with your living immortal beyond your assigned position within the clan. You are forbidden from being assigned as Consort by your living immortal or her Steward, current or future. Violation of any of these three items will lead to immediate removal from your clan. You will be considered a rogue and will be put to death. Do you understand the sentence I have placed upon you?"

Worse than death. That was what Joseph had said. He knew this was an option. Chatelain must have mentioned something or perhaps he had been forced to lose something or someone he loved too.

"I understand."

"Your full sentence will be sent to your clan's Steward for their records. Your living immortal will be forbidden from knowing the details until your immortal life is over."

"I understand."

Keeping Arabella in the dark ensured that the decision would be mine to make, or not. She would not be punished but my immortal life would end. If her hatred was as deep as I believed, anything other than indifference was the best I could ever expect anyway.

Tsu nodded and the Council rose. They filed out to the far left of the stage and around a corner, with the exception of Tsu who walked toward me. She handed me a thick envelope from within her robes.

"Your current accommodations are needed immediately for another." She tapped the envelope against her other hand. "The gate and elevator codes are inside, as is a list of Council approved hotels. Your expertise is required for another ongoing infraction. Return here three weeks from now at eleven and we will begin. Details have been left with your belongings."

"Thank you." I accepted the envelope but did not look inside.

She nodded then continued, "The remaining items that were previously denied and the overlooked materials are already in your room. A vehicle has been assigned for use for the remainder of your stay."

I quickly gathered my things and turned to leave when she called out. "Remember, Victor, you work for us now and we will be keeping a close eye on you."

Without turning back, I strode out of the room and toward my freedom, as temporary as it may be. The hallway was empty when I opened the door. No more babysitter. I was being left to either follow the Council's sentence or speed my death.

* * *

I wasted no time gathering my few belongings, including a new cell phone and laptop. The banker boxes were gone but when I opened the laptop, there was a file folder which I assumed were electronic versions. There was also an untitled document which I hoped contained the details on the infraction I was supposed to review. I smiled when I saw the two paperbacks remained.

A key fob sat beside the books. I packed them and stuffed the key in my pocket and headed in the direction that I thought was the parking garage. After walking around for twenty minutes, I finally found it.

I pressed the fob and heard a faint "bloop". I walked in the direction of the sound and pressed it again. The headlights on the dark blue Tesla S flashed. Now this was the kind of treatment I was used to.

The car was silent as I pulled from the underground garage. I didn't go far before I saw a sign for the interstate. This time of night, there were very few cars so I took advantage and put the pedal down. Weaving between the semis was too easy. Weeks of tension rolled off my shoulders as the world passed in the blur.

A sign for the airport caught my eye as I sped past. The idea of leaving this all behind made my foot ease up. Was it worth one more night, one more minute with her? A letter was one thing but I wanted to tell Arabella everything in person, to see the reaction in her eyes for myself.

The cell phone chimed in the passenger seat and I slowed to check the message. *The car has a tracker.*

Of course, it did. There were probably only a few people with this number and only one who would try to help me. I took the next exit and headed back toward the city. Once downtown, I drove until I found a bar.

"Last call in fifteen," the bartender called as I entered.

"Top shelf whiskey with a whiskey chaser."

He chuckled and grabbed two glasses. The young woman at the door looked at my ID and gave me a shy smile. I considered it for about half a second then moved on. The rest of the place was empty except for two heavily tattooed guys deep in conversation at the other end of the bar.

I took out the envelope and scanned the hotel options. Nothing stood out so I used my phone to find the one closest to the temple. I downed both whiskeys and left a fifty on the bar.

The valet looked a little too excited when I handed over the key but it wasn't mine, not really, so what did I care if he took it on a little joy ride. Let the Council chase him around for a few hours instead of me. The guy at the front desk barely looked awake when I approached.

"I need a suite," I said, pulling out my wallet.

He yawned. "Do you have a reservation?"

A very attractive dark-haired woman with shockingly blue eyes came through a door behind the desk as I spoke, "No, but I'm here on Council business."

She smiled brightly and nudged the sleepy man. "I've got this Evan. Go take your break." She took my ID and tapped on the keyboard with her long red nails. "Mr. River. We've been expecting you. You're on the top floor. The private elevator is through the lobby to the left."

I took the electronic keys she slid across the counter. "Thank you."

She didn't let go right away and when I looked up, she held my gaze and licked her lips. "I'll be here all night if you need anything. You can ask for me specifically."

I glanced at her name tag. "Thank you again, Sylvie."

The room was a standard two-room suite. Nothing special but at least I could come and go as I pleased. I put the laptop on the small table and pulled the phone from my pocket.

If the car had a tracker and I was staying as a 'guest' in a Council approved hotel, I was willing to bet the room was bugged. I wasn't allowed to communicate with Arabella or Rowan but I knew one person who could answer a few questions. Plus, an apology was in order.

"Hello?" a sleepy voice answered.

"Eve, it's me."

The phone made a garbled noise and I assumed she had dropped it. "Oh my God, Victor! Are you okay? Where are you? When are you coming back? Everything is such a mess here."

"I'm fine, sis. And I'm sorry for dragging you into all this."

"Pfft. Those are the least of my troubles. My girlfriend is now undead, the new semester is killing me, and I've been worried sick about you and um…" She let the sentence die but I knew what she was going to say.

"It's going to be a while before I can come back. I have a job to finish but I promise I *am* coming back. I didn't think about how late it was but could you bring me up to speed on what's going on there?"

I felt myself slipping back into the selfish prick the Council had made me see. If I was being listened to, Eve was my best source of information as long as I worded my questions carefully. I promised myself that I would make it up to her.

"Where to even start? Acacia dropped out of school for obvious reasons. Arabella broke off the engagement with Tom but she's not really telling me why, which is really annoying. Tom was living with me for a couple weeks but is now in California getting ready to start the tour that was postponed. Mom is pissed about the whole kid thing. Oh my gosh, you don't even know about that! Tom has an eight-year-old with his ex. He's so cute. I love being an aunt." She ended with a yawn.

Arabella had broken it off? I wonder if it was because of the boy. My mind began to drift toward other reasons but I shut it down. I'd used up all my luck. The best I could hope for was her continued acceptance as part of the clan. The thought made my chest ache.

"Are you still there?" Eve asked.

"Yeah. I'm here." There were so many things I needed to know and no way to ask. "I'm going to let you go back to sleep, Eve. Save this number. Love you, sis."

"Love you too. Happy Valentine's Day."

When the phone went dead, I looked at the screen. It was Valentine's Day. The solitude in the basement really made me lose track of time. Stupid commercial holiday anyway but…

I pulled up the text I'd received earlier about the car and silently prayed it was Joseph.

I need a favor. Send a gift box of hot chocolate to my living immortal. No card necessary.

While I wasn't allowed to communicate with them, no one told me my liaison couldn't. She'd know it was from me. She'd have to. The letter I'd written to her popped into my head and I quickly sent another text.

Don't mail the letter.

The reply was almost instant. *It was sent before your sentence so no rules were broken.*

I tossed the phone on the bed and turned on the laptop. The cursor hovered over the untitled document. With a double click, it opened. *Seraphine Chatelain* was the first line. How the hell was I supposed to be an impartial third party to that bitch? I guess this was my chance to show the Immortal Council they could trust me.

Chapter Thirty

Curiosity kept me focused on the files and details of Seraphine's case for the first week or so. I felt like I was back in law school but this was my ticket to real freedom. The Immortal Council, or more likely Chatelain, left out more than a few boxes after my initial request. There were hundreds more pages of both immortal and living immortal statutes. If I'd had access to these earlier, I may have actually had decent closing arguments for my own sentencing, not that it would have mattered. I got lucky. Now, it was my job to make sure Seraphine didn't.

Whenever my mind wandered, I checked Eve's social media pages. I had to scroll through a lot of recipes and fashion posts to find what I wanted. There were only a couple pictures of Eve and Acacia, even fewer including Arabella. Some were at Eve's condo, most were somewhere I didn't recognize. My guess was the house the Council had given to Arabella.

Arabella's smile didn't quite reach her eyes. She looked like she was going through the motions but her heart wasn't in whatever fun they were supposed to be having. There was one image of Eve showing off a new dress; Arabella's profile had been caught in the background. Her posture was defiant; clearly, she was arguing with whomever she was talking to.

My hand reached for my phone but I closed it into a fist. This radio silence was torture, not that I truly believed she would take my call anyway. Eve had been in constant communication but her texts contained nothing of substance. They were vague and sometimes disjointed enough that I began to wonder if my messages were being censored.

My next stop was an online tabloid. I'd been reduced to this as my sole source for updates on Tom and his new life. There was no solid reason I couldn't call him; I just wasn't ready for that conversation yet. It was a good thing he was states away because I really wanted to make him pay for putting me in this situation, and more importantly breaking Arabella's heart. The photos and articles painted a picture of domestic bliss with Rachel and his son. It made me sick. I'd never hated him more.

The knock on my door was probably a Godsend. I glanced at the clock, quarter past ten, and I slapped the lid down on the laptop in disgust. Joseph stood outside my door and it was just the distraction I needed.

I pulled on my shoes and opened the door. "Let's go."

Sometimes I liked Joseph's silence. He didn't feel pressured to fill time with small talk or useless chatter. Just before I pulled the door closed, I tossed my cell back onto the bed. I needed a break from everything. It was exhausting trying to ignore my own life.

"Don't you ever go anywhere else?" I asked when Joseph pulled the door open to the same restaurant we'd visited multiple times.

"I'm comfortable here."

Marty gave us an enthusiastic wave as the hostess took us to his section. Even his normal, annoying happiness was a welcome change. We ordered our usual and I watched the fire.

Joseph finally broke the comfortable silence. "Would you like to hear a joke?"

"Never in a million years would I expect those words to come out of your mouth. Lay it on me."

"Santa Claus, the tooth fairy, an honest lawyer, and an old drunk are walking down the street together when they simultaneously spot a hundred-dollar bill. Who gets it?"

I took a long drink of wine, trying to come up with the punchline. "I give up but feel like I'm going to regret the answer."

"The old drunk, of course! The other three are fantasy creatures."

"Ouch." I chuckled. "I thought we were friends."

Joseph laughed a bit harder than necessary. It wasn't that funny but his mood was helping to lift mine. Somehow, I doubted he had a lot of down time to really be himself.

"I have one more."

"After that, I'm sure you have more than one."

"The lawyer says to the judge, 'my client is trapped in a penny.' The judge asks, 'he's what?'"

"Wait! I know this one." Marty appeared at that moment. "The lawyer says, 'He's in a cent.'"

The two of them fell into hysterics. I drained my glass and took the refill from Marty. This was going to be a long night but clearly it was what I needed. For the first time in recent memory, I just let myself enjoy the moment.

* * *

We agreed to meet once a week and I welcomed the break. I also visited the homeless shelter with Joseph on several more occasions. Doing for others without wanting anything in return was something the old me would have never considered. I was getting the blood I needed but if they hadn't offered, I could have found it elsewhere. Jingtao was trying to teach me Mandarin and I was terrible at it, which made her laugh. It felt nice to be part of something other than my own misery.

The nights seemed to speed by and suddenly it was time to face the Immortal Council and Seraphine again. I had to bury my loathing for both if I was ever going to get out of here.

A new file mysteriously appeared on the laptop yesterday morning. It just reinforced the idea that while I was left to my own devices, everything I did was being observed. The file held the final information for the meeting tonight.

The Council would be run by Tsu as acting leader. Chatelain would be present but not as a voting member. There was something extremely satisfying about him having to see me in my element but being forced to keep his mouth shut.

A new custom-made suit was part of the preparation. Sylvie had arranged for the tailor to come to me. It arrived yesterday and I couldn't be more pleased with the result. The jet-black jacket and slacks paired nicely with a deep purple and black pinstripe shirt. I'd ordered a navy suit too but hoped I wouldn't need it.

Joseph was waiting outside the auditorium when I arrived. His expression was all business. He nodded in my direction but didn't speak. This may be the last time we saw each other. I should have said something but no words came.

I pulled the door open and descended the stairs. The space was equally impactful as the first time but the scene in front of me had changed. Both the Immortal Council and the accused were set up on the stage. That made sense. In their eyes, Seraphine was an equal. I was decidedly not.

Seraphine was dressed in all white, looking downright angelic, except for the fact she was in a large metal cage. She sat primly on a purple high-backed chair, feet crossed at the ankles. Her eyes were downcast as in submission. I didn't buy it for one second.

The council members were split between two large tables, next to each were four chairs. Chatelain sat on the end closest to his daughter. Only the chair farthest from him and set somewhat apart from the rest, remained open. Logic suggested that was for me. I aimed for the seat and set my laptop and other materials on the table.

Gutierrez held the seat next to mine. He gave me a professional smile and nodded in welcome. No one else even acknowledged my arrival. They continued to chat amongst themselves as if it were a garden party.

After several pain-staking minutes, Tsu moved to silence the chatter. She glanced at Gutierrez to confirm he was ready to record the session. At his affirmative response, she began.

The acoustics of the room gave her voice a power beyond her demure appearance. "Seraphine Chatelain, living immortal and daughter of Pierre Chatelain, you are here today to answer for your crimes against the Immortal Council, your fellow living immortals, and the vows you've broken toward your own reborn. Do you understand these charges?"

Seraphine's head bobbed up and down in agreement followed by a very small, "Yes."

I'd reviewed the numerous crimes for which she would be answering today. Everything from murder of a dozen living immortals, countless of her own reborn, all the way down to refusal to attend Council mandated gatherings and something about failure to meet the hosting requirements. The latter I skimmed in passing. I knew they wanted all the infractions listed but some were just a waste of time. The first of her crimes only had one possible outcome. Death.

Chatelain stood, approached his daughter, then turned back to face the Council. "I would like to say a few words before Seraphine speaks."

"Proceed," Tsu permitted.

He swept his arm wide in a grandiose fashion as if we hadn't already seen the elaborate cage. "This treatment of a living immortal is deplorable and beneath us. While she has clearly made some egregious mistakes, she is not an animal. Her life is precious and the gift she can give is not something to be wasted. I have taken full responsibility for her actions as it was my blind eye that allowed them to occur. I've stepped down as Council Leader but will serve as they see fit. Do not lay judgment hastily. She is but a child and needs guidance."

I glanced at my notes. A three-hundred-year-old child, beaten to death by the very man who championed for her now. And I thought my family was fucked up.

Pierre continued to regale the Council with more of her unique and special qualities. "The Immortal Council was created to protect our living immortals. Today, we are less than one hundred strong. To lose another," he paused and glanced my way before continuing, "would be a sacrifice too great to bear."

And there it was. The real reason I was here. He had manipulated the Council into including me as a defense tool to spare his daughter's life. They would look at me and be reminded that I too had murdered a living immortal, lessening their total numbers and jeopardizing their reason for being.

I let him break eye contact first. If he wanted a fight, I'd give him one. So far, he'd only seen the man with nothing left to lose. Now, he'd see one who had everything to live for.

Chapter Thirty-One

The Council gave Seraphine the floor next. She slid gently off the chair, smoothed her ankle length dress then folded her hands together. Her icy blue gaze moved slowly from one face to the next until she met mine. I swear I saw a hint of a smile but I may have imagined it. While her father was easy to read due to his astonishing arrogance, she was a master manipulator in her subtlety.

"Thank you for giving me a chance to speak." Her voice was soft and even. "My childhood was stolen from me and I was thrust into a world for which I wasn't prepared. The Council attempted to provide guidance but with no support other than the constant reminder of my unique gifts, I made decisions with only myself in mind. They were the wrong ones but as a child, I continued to create a world I felt was right for me. Over the years, I lost my way and turned my back on the Council as I thought they had abandoned me."

She wiped a tear away before she continued. God, she was good. "I am guilty of all you claim. I need help to do what is right. All I ask is one chance to be better and make amends for the wrongs I've done."

The expressions of the council members ranged from disgust to sympathy. Seraphine's cherubic appearance was her best defense. Her words were probably sprinkled with the truth but ultimately, she was using her innocent visage to sway emotions in her favor. No matter what I said, I was picking sides or rather I would make the Council choose one.

Tsu turned to me. "Mr. River, you have been asked here to provide a neutral third-party perspective on these charges. As such, you are a representative of the Council, any retaliation or offense against you will be considered an affront to the Council itself. You were provided with the laws in which we will use to decide and administer punishment. What options have you prepared?"

I stood and walked between the Council and Seraphine. "Thank you, Leader Tsu and the rest of the Council for this opportunity. My history with the accused is well known, but today is not about those recent events. This is about years of blatant disregard of the very laws by which all immortals are sworn. Living immortals are held to even higher standards as they are revered above all else. Seraphine was indeed a child when her immortal life began. However, she was given the same resources, perhaps more due to her family ties, as all other living immortals. Instead of joining the community meant to serve and protect her, Seraphine turned her back to create a world of her own in which she answered to no one.

These crimes were then ignored by the very leader of the institution to which she disowned. The leader who in making her immortal at such a young age never gave her the chance to be prepared or to understand the consequences of her actions. The very same man who in making her immortal at such a young age never gave her the chance to create future living immortals."

Several council members leaned into their neighbors to whisper. This was clearly not the path they expected me to walk. I stopped in front of Chatelain and let the words sink in. Hatred like I'd never seen burned in his eyes. This man was never going to be on my side and would never trust my judgment on Council related matters. As long as he held any sort of power, my life and, more importantly, the lives of the people I cared about were in jeopardy.

"Council, please." Tsu's voice rose above the din. "Mr. Rivers, continue."

I nodded and began a slow walk back to my seat. "The laws are very clear that premeditated murder of a living immortal is death, no matter who strikes the final blow. Living immortals, while held to that higher standard, are exempt in many aspects of Council law. However, this is not one of those cases. After reviewing all the materials, there are only two options to be considered."

My pause was long enough that Tsu spoke again. "And those options are?"

"The Immortal Council must decide who is more responsible for the crimes committed by Seraphine." I let out a slow breath. "The accused or her father."

The uproar was exactly what I expected. The only two silent figures in the room were Seraphine and Pierre. I'd just signed my death warrant but who would come to collect?

* * *

Once Tsu was able to regain order over the Council, she dismissed me, Chatelain, and ordered Seraphine be removed from the auditorium temporarily during deliberations. The three of us left in different directions.

The area outside the auditorium was not empty but Joseph was nowhere to be seen. I waited a few minutes then found a seat and checked my phone. There was a message from Eve.

I had a weird feeling and just wanted to make sure you were okay.

I reread the text and her previous ones as I thought about how to reply. The messages were definitely getting censored. I'd need to get a replacement phone soon.

I'm fine. Hopefully coming back soon. I'm in meetings tonight. I'll try to call you tomorrow.

Bubbles immediately popped up as she typed a reply. *Yay! I'll tell everyone.*

I said hopefully *but yes, you can tell them.*

The door opened about an hour later and I was motioned back inside by Councilman Young. He'd been pretty neutral in all our meetings so his appearance gave nothing away.

Chatelain and Seraphine stood side by side on the stage. A group of men in black suits stood in a semi-circle behind them like prison guards. I quickly moved back to my seat.

When Tsu stood to address the Council, her face looked strained. "With heavy hearts, the Council has reached a decision. Living immortals are becoming more and more rare. We cannot risk losing anymore. That being said, without order there is chaos."

I had to hide my smile when I realized Seraphine's own clan motto was taken directly from the Council. There was no chance it was a coincidence. She probably knew more about the laws and restrictions than most of the council members and used it to her advantage.

Tsu turned her back to the Council and spoke to both of the accused. "Your actions will have consequences far beyond your own lives. The Immortal Council has been operating under an outdated set of conventions. The events being reviewed here today show us just how much. You have thrust us all forward into change, whether that was or was not your intent.

Seraphine Chatelain, you have asked for help, and help you will receive. You will rotate between all council member's clans until they see legitimate progress in your rehabilitation. No matter how long that takes. Your immortal clan will be reassigned until you have proven yourself worthy. You will not be allowed to create any new reborn until this restriction has been lifted. Your life is to be spared but, there will be no more chances. If you forget, ignore, or even think about stepping outside the boundaries set by the Council, you will be immediately dispatched. There will be no defense or further discussion. Do you understand the sentence in which you have received?"

Seraphine let out a slow breath. "I understand, Council Leader Tsu."

Next to his daughter, Chatelain's expression turned sour. Hearing his title being used on another must be like salt in a wound. He knew my words had damned him, even if they had saved his child. I'd either split them further apart or given them reason to work together.

Tsu turned to face him. "Pierre Chatelain, your words and actions on behalf of your living immortal daughter have been heard and considered. As such, your duties for the Immortal Council will be suspended until further notice. You will retain leadership of your clan but travel outside your boundaries are restricted. The progress of Seraphine's rehabilitation will directly affect your own integration back into immortal society. Do you understand the sentence in which you have received?"

Chatelain adjusted his stance. "I do, Councilwoman Tsu."

If Tsu noticed the title, she didn't react. "Pierre, you will be escorted back to your lodgings and will depart for your home territory at once. Seraphine, you will return to your rooms until a schedule for rotation through the Council has been completed."

Tsu turned back to the Council and adjourned the meeting. Her eyes locked with mine and I knew I wasn't going anywhere for a while.

Epilogue

"I'm sorry, sis. I can't give you any idea of when I'll be back." I told Eve for the third time.

"But you said soon," she almost whined.

"No, I said 'hopefully soon'. There are some things I need to wrap up here. I'll be back before you know it."

"Could I come visit you?"

I tapped a pen against my desk. Multiple windows were open on the laptop and I'd added a second and third monitor. Tsu had given me a new task immediately after the sentencing of the Chatelains. This would not be an easy one and I would need to take my time. For the first time in a long while, time was on my side.

The Immortal Council positions had been held by the same members for centuries. The process for appointment was kill or be killed. That policy was no longer. All current council members would be replaced, with the exclusion of the acting leader. A lottery system would be put into place. Once the new seven were chosen, they would vote amongst themselves as who the Council Leader would be. The lottery appointment would last no more than fifty years.

There were other stipulations in place, such as age of living immortal and size of clan. With fewer than one hundred current living immortals total, some of the current members would most likely return to their stations. The Chatelain line was currently being excluded as part of the larger sentence against Pierre and Seraphine.

This exception was fine by me. Arabella needed time to acclimate to this new future. Her entire world was in upheaval. Council reform shouldn't be part of that, even though it would ultimately continue to shape her life.

A life I would be a part of. It may not have been what I wanted but I would be there as part of her clan. For whatever reason, she had not turned her back on me. When I started on my path to immortality, my own selfish gains were my only goal. Now, I planned on spending the rest of my existence trying to make this world everything she needed.

"I'm pretty busy but I bet I can make time for my favorite sister. Let me make a call and we'll get you a plane ticket."

"Eve, the movie is about to start." I heard Arabella's voice in the background and my breath caught.

"Have a good night, sis. I love you."

"Love you, Victor. See you soon."

About the Author

Melinda Call grew up in the Pacific Northwest and Mountain West of the United States. She loves her family fiercely, even the four-legged ones that don't speak clearly. Her hobbies include reading, gardening, and baking. Feeding the people she cares about is her love language. She talks too much and cries during almost every movie/TV show/commercial that she doesn't fall asleep watching. Even though she is a scientist by day, she whole-heartedly believes magic exists.

Check out Melinda's website, https://melindacall.com, to read about her crazy life, books, freebies, and for links to follow her on social media.

Make sure to sign up for her newsletter so you never miss any big announcements.

Other Books by Melinda Call

Blood Target Part 1 and 2, prequel to *Blood Match.* Link for the free download on Melinda's website.

Blood Match, Book One of the Blood Match Series. Purchase eBook or paperback at your favorite retailers.

www.ingramcontent.com/pod-product-compliance
Lightning Source LLC
LaVergne TN
LVHW050616100826
845148LV00011B/1606

* 9 7 9 8 9 8 8 3 7 6 7 5 0 *